"*The Sacred Sermon* was a true Nicolle Pierce. As the senior pa have been put on notice that I am to protect and teach my members, not devour them like wolves to satisfy my "manly" desires. This book, while fiction, gave me a revelational glimpse into the confusion, pain and ultimate destruction of lives my irresponsibility can cause if I were to fall. *The Sacred Sermon* is a must read for all...sheep and shepherds."

Pastor Andre "AJ" Jones

Amen Fellowship Church, Houston, TX

"This book is by far my favorite book besides the Bible, so that is saying a lot. I enjoyed reading this book. I could relate to the book. When I started reading the book, thinking I was just going to read a few chapters I could not put it down and did not put it down until I was finished. I cannot wait until the sequel."

Tabitha S. Burroughs

Duncanville, TX

"*The Sacred Sermon* has been a best seller with Jokae's African American Bookstore since its release. We have sold over a thousand copies to customers who are anxious for the sequel. It is a novel that has truly touched all that have had the pleasure to read it."

Til Pettis, Owner

Jokae's African American Bookstore, Dallas, TX

"This was a great read and story line! I finished this book in one day. I would highly recommend this book. It is sprinkled with prayers and scripture, but not too much that you would think that this is a Christian novel, but enough to know that a Christ centered person wrote it."

Tannie McGregor, President

Cover2Cover Book Club

Houston, TX

Publisher's Note

This book is a work of fiction. Any names, characters, places and incidents are either the product of the author's imagination or are used fictitiously and any resemblance to actual persons, living or dead, business establishments, events or locales are strictly coincidental.

The Sacred Sermon

Published by Pierce Publishing
© 2004 Nicolle Pierce
All Rights Reserved

Pierce Publishing Company
40 FM 1960 West
Suite 244
Houston, TX 77090

www.thesacredsermon.com
email:sacredsermon@nicollepierce.com

The Sacred Sermon
By Nicolle Pierce

ISBN 0-9755748-0-9

Printed in United States of America

Third Printing December, 2005

Dedication

This Book Is Dedicated
To The Memory Of:

Charles Edward Pierce

The greatest dad that ever lived!

Acknowledgements

Thank you, Lord, for the vision, strength, and perseverance needed to complete this project. You are my Alpha and Omega and worthy to be praised.

I wish to thank my mother, Berdie Pierce, who always challenged and encouraged me to reach my goals. I love you, Mama, and it is my hope to continue to make you proud.

My sister and brother-in-law, Tonya & Kevin, helped purchase the computer I used to birth out the vision God gave to me. I am forever grateful for that and all that you have done with helping me complete my journey.

My supportive Godparents, Rev. Donald and Faye Wallace, I appreciate all of your love and support.

Stephney Thomas, Andrea Lavely, Dr. Freddie Wade III, Tamika Martin, Phoebe Evans, LaTonya Hopkins, Kelvin Love, Porsha Nealy, Joycelyn Vann-Whitten, and Dennis Scroggins have been my support and encouragement through this journey and definitely fueled me on days I was running out of gas.

To the hundreds of readers who have blessed me with letters, emails and reviews, I have no words that can express my appreciation for your support. You are the reason for my words.

And a special thank you to the entire Leffall and Pierce families.

You are all angels sent by God and I love you dearly.

Foreword

It was after midnight, and I still had seventeen more hours before I would get to Texas. I had wanted to get on the road earlier, but the movers were late picking up my furniture, which put me behind schedule. Even though people thought I was crazy, I was determined to make the haul from New York to Dallas without stopping. I felt the time it took for me to get a hotel room, unwind, shower, eat and sleep would only delay my arrival to my new life.

After going over the Delaware Memorial Bridge, I made a quick stop at a shopping center right off I-95. I walked into a Barnes and Noble seconds before they locked the door for the night. I quickly purchased three of Iyanla Vanzant's self-help tapes and two Danielle Steele audio novels to keep my mind occupied. Besides, if the tapes didn't do the job, my *NO DOZE* and coffee I bought at the Diamond Shamrock would.

As I returned to my car, refreshed from my thirty minutes of stretching my legs and clearing my head, I faced the next thousand miles with anticipation. Import Sales Incorporated had recently promoted me to account area manager of the Texas market. As one of the largest direct advertising and sales companies in North America, they had high expectations of penetrating the Texas market to create more business and higher margins on existing customers. I started there over two years ago and eventually led a sales force of fifty to setting a company record of opening over a thousand new accounts within a year. That was a record they hoped I could duplicate.

After my first Iyanla tape, I needed a break. Even though I loved my self-help, audio books, I had all I could take. I rolled down the window of my Mazda MX6 to allow the cool, dark October air to hit my face. I was able to find a midnight love station and heard Freddie Jackson crooning, "You are my Lady. You're everything I need and more…" As I listened to the words, I couldn't avoid several thoughts of the recent past from entering my head.

As I crossed the Maryland State line, I realized this was going to be a long drive. My butt was already sore. I shifted my weight to one side, and in doing so, was reminded of my desperate need to make a new start. I felt a discharge of blood from between my legs, finding its way to my maxi-pad. I had made so many mistakes — big, huge mistakes. Mistakes and memories I knew I could not shake easily without a fresh start in a new city with new people and no reminders.

I had been discharging blood for the last two days. The cramping had stopped for the most part, but when I felt them returning, I would pop a couple of my prescription pain relievers. Someone once said that God makes abortions hurt so much to punish you for killing one of his children. Another "expert" said that the pain mirrors the pain of the unborn child during termination. I'd never experienced anything like it. It's a pain I would not wish on anyone. The cold, hard surgical devices, the nervousness and the pure agony of the scraping of flesh from my womb were almost too much to bear. As bad as it was, it couldn't compare to the emotional scars I now have because I chose to terminate a pregnancy, not once, but twice. I had become pregnant and aborted two babies. The father was my pastor, Reverend Kevin Lewis.

Chapter 1

Two Years Earlier

It was snowing lightly this windy October day in 1996. I sped into the parking lot to what was to be my first Delta Sigma Theta meeting in Chicago. I was looking forward to meeting my local sorors and being part of a network of positive black women. I parked the car and quickly walked to the main entrance of the small church. The building reminded me of the old church my grandfather pastored in Marshall, TX. It wasn't one of those small, country, one-room churches, but would not be considered a mega-church, either. The tall building was constructed with red brick, which was offset by a set of white double doors leading to the main entryway facing the street. The fact that the parking lot was gravel instead of cement really reminded me of the days of visiting Papa's church.

After battling the high winds and finally reaching the double doors, I turned the cold, gold handle and pulled. "Damn, it's locked." There were cars in the parking lot, so I knew they were in there. I ran around to the side door and knocked. No answer. I knocked again, but with more force, and eventually heard steps approaching, then the unlocking of the door. As the door opened, I was taken off guard when I made eye contact with one of the most handsome men I had ever seen. He was every bit of 6'4" with smooth hershey-brown skin, dark wavy hair, and a beautiful smile, which displayed the whitest teeth behind the sexiest lips, I had seen in a long time. He was dressed in a black tee shirt and Levis loose-fitting jeans. Who was he?

"Are you here for the Delta meeting?" His voice was deep and professional.

"Yes, I'm a few minutes late, but…"

"Not a problem, I think they just started a few minutes ago. They're upstairs." He interrupted, sensing I was pressed for time.

The handsome stranger led me to a stairway, and then disappeared.

1

The meeting was in progress when I entered the room. Not wanting to draw attention to my tardiness, I took the first seat I could find in the rear of the mid-sized room. An attractive young soror sporting fashionable dreads mouthed hello as I sat down. After forty-five minutes of hearing the old business, new business, plans, procedures, and policies, it was all over. Before the meeting adjourned we gathered in a circle, held hands and sang our Delta song.

A few sorors came up to me afterwards to introduce themselves. I came to realize my sorors had it going on. I met a number of educators, attorneys, and business professionals.

Soror Hazel Walker, a beautiful, older woman in her late fifties, really seemed to take an interest in me. She asked me what I did for a living and when I told her I had a career as a communications specialist she seemed impressed and asked how I got into the field. When I mentioned to her that I graduated from Tuskegee University with a degree in marketing, her face lit up.

"Well, I should have known there was something special about you," she said, wearing a mischievous smile.

"What?"

"Well, I'm a 1958 graduate of Tuskegee Institute. I pledged Delta in 1956."

"Oh, my God, no way!" I screamed, hugging her, feeling even more connected.

"I have to admit, I wish they would rename it Tuskegee Institute. I just never really liked University. But nevertheless, I'm so glad you're an alumnus. Have you been back to a homecoming recently?" she asked.

"I went back the year after I graduated, but not since. I would like to return next year, though."

"I'm taking my granddaughter next year. I've been pushing for her to choose Tuskegee. She's a senior next year and she's trying to decide between Tuskegee and Spelman. Hopefully, she'll make the right choice."

"I'm sure if you have anything to do with it, she will," I kidded while winking an eye.

She asked me if I was from Chicago originally and when I told her I had only been living here for five months she invited me to her church.

"Where is your church? I still haven't mastered my way around Chicago too well," I asked, flattered she would invite me.

"You're in it. We have wonderful services here and we would love to have you come visit with us," the senior soror said, smiling up at me.

"Well, I'll definitely visit. Thank you so much for the invitation. What time do services start?"

"11:00," she said, smiling at me.

"I'll be here this coming Sunday. Thanks again, I appreciate it."

*　*　*

Looking out my window, it was a Hallelujah Sunday morning. The sun beamed across the sky as if ten thousands angels sang the rays to life. The light snow had stopped, but judging from the way the wind was swaying the trees, it was brisk. I was wearing a red silk blouse, a long, black wrapped skirt, sheer black panty hose and my new black Nine West pumps. As I checked myself out in the mirror, I had to admit I looked nice. As soon as I gave myself the stamp of approval, I wondered what my motives were. There was no doubting I was saved and I definitely loved the Lord, but there had to be some eligible men at this church. Maybe even the mystery doorman I met just a few days earlier.

As I pulled into the parking lot of the church, I noticed there were only a few cars there, maybe twelve. Was I early? I checked my watch. It was 11:17am. I entered the front door of the church and was greeted and given a church program of the day's service by a young boy who had to be around ten. Waiting for the church doors to open, I had a feeling of warmth. I could give the credit to the heat the church provided, after coming out of the brisk air, but there was something else. There was a warm spirit in this place. Peering into the church through the square window in the brown, wooden door separating the entryway from the church, I could see the burgundy pews and golden decorations throughout the sacred room. Behind the pulpit and choir stand hung a massive, golden cross that commanded attention. Strangely enough, the whole setting wasn't consistent with how I thought it would look, judging from the exterior and the small room where the Delta meeting was held. Three middle-aged men started singing "Guide me over, thy great Jehovah..." At that time a young white couple in their early twenties entered and gave a bright, welcoming smile and said good morning. About a minute later, the church doors swung open and some of the congregation looked back to see who was coming in. I sat on the fourth row from the rear next to a young black girl holding what appeared to be her newborn baby.

A very old, yet stylish woman of about eighty who later introduced herself as Sister Lula Mae Moon approached the podium at the front of the church and started reading the announcements, sick and shut ins, and prayer list in her old, rattled voice. Then she came to the subject I always dreaded when I visited smaller churches — the visitors. They always want you to stand and say something. "Will all our visitors please stand and state your name and church home?"

Normally, I have a few minutes to think about what I am going to say, but because I had only sat down sixty seconds before, I was caught off guard. I stood because a church this small had already spotted you as a visitor and I would feel worse just to sit there and have the whole church look at me with that "Aren't you a visitor?" look.

I rose with another woman who was seated a few pews up. Luckily, she went first. The fashionably dressed, middle-aged lady

4

wearing a huge hat stated she was from Oakland, California and was in town visiting her grandson LaDeonte (or something like that). There were a few applauds and amens from church members who supposedly knew the grandson with the ugly name. All I know is it bought me some time to figure out what I was going to say.

It was now my turn and the whole church was staring at me. My heart skipped a beat and my mouth dried to the point where I swear I could grow cotton in it. I quickly scanned the small crowd and was shocked to see my handsome doorman on the front row! Seeing him temporarily messed my head up to the point where I lost my thoughts on what I had prepared to say.

I took a deep breath and gushed out, "Good morning, my name is Natalie Thomas and I recently moved here from Cleveland, Ohio. It's a pleasure to worship with you today."

The congregation said, "Amen."

"Here at Divine Baptist Church we would like to extend our warmest welcome to you and if you are ever in need of a church home, we would love to have you join our church family. God bless you and please come again." Sister Lula Mae Moon then slowly crept her way back to her seat.

My mind was now occupied with two thoughts. *Did I sound stupid?* And more importantly, *Did I sound stupid to my handsome doorman?*

The youth choir, which looked like it consisted of kids from age three to fifteen, sang, "Jesus Loves Me". The dramatic age and size difference of the eight children looked awkward, but I suppose it was a direct reflection of the church size. In a church with more members, there would be a children and youth choir.

I looked to see my handsome doorman on the front row and saw no Mrs. Doorman. He looked good, even better than our first encounter. His hair looked freshly cut and even my rear view could detect unprocessed waves which were rich and dark. He was wearing a dark colored suit that gave him a more polished appearance than before. There's just something about a man in a suit.

As the choir finished, I noticed that my doorman rose from his seat and stepped onto the pulpit. What was he doing?

"Amen, amen. Children are definitely a gift from God and they just sang like the angels they are."

No, it can't be. My tall, handsome doorman was the pastor?

"If you will now open your Bibles to John, Chapter three, verse two..."

As he started his sermon, I found him to be very articulate and educated with his delivery. The way he pronounced each syllable in every word, the colorful analogies he applied to the scriptures and the way he didn't "hoot," but executed his sermon as a professional orator or motivational speaker was something I had never seen in any other preacher.

After the benediction, he stood at the doorway of the church shaking everyone's hands as they exited. While I stood in line, I secretly slipped an Altoid to freshen my breath, licked my teeth to remove any unwanted lipstick, and swept my hair behind one ear to prepare for my up close and personal encounter.

He was only two people away from me when I saw him notice me and smile. I looked away and the butterflies started fluttering overtime. He looked 6'4, 200 pounds, around thirty-five and extremely together. That was an expensive suit he was wearing, too. I could tell by the way it fit his body. He was also wearing cuff links — gold ones!! I love a man in cuff links.

"Sister..." he paused, "I'm sorry, what is your name again?"

"Natalie... Natalie Thomas, excuse me, umm, Sister Natalie Thomas." I couldn't believe I gave the pastor my first name, that couldn't be holy, not only that, I was stumbling over my words, he probably couldn't even understand what I said.

"Did you enjoy the service, Sister Thomas?" He asked smiling, noticing I had a hard time keeping it together.

"Yes, I definitely did," I said as I smiled and broke eye contact. I couldn't bear to look at him. He was so handsome.

"That's good. Sister Thomas, I hope you will visit us again. Did you mention if you had a church home?"

"No, unfortunately I don't, but I will be visiting again." I had visited several churches and none had left me feeling spiritually fed, but I didn't feel the need to say all of that. My tongue was not cooperating with my brain. I needed to keep everything short and simple.

"We would love to have you. Have a blessed week."

"I will. Thank you."

Chapter 2

For the next two months I attended Divine Baptist Church and was loving the services. I even started going to Bible study on Wednesday nights. It was great because I felt I was getting the best of both worlds. I had established an involvement with a growing church that was teaching and preaching the word of God. The icing on the cake was that it just happened to be led by Pastor Kevin Lewis, the best looking man I had seen in a long time.

About a week later, I made the decision to join. Since attending church and bible study on a regular basis, I felt I had really grown spiritually and I did need a church home. So, when the doors of the church would open for new members this coming Sunday, I would stride down that aisle.

I chose a moderately sexy, yet classy black, wrap dress, with sheer, black pantyhose and black, sling-back shoes. I topped off the outfit with a simple, yet elegant necklace with matching bracelet my dad had given me for my twenty-fifth birthday.

I sat next to Sister Walker who had saved me a seat the last few Sundays. During service she would pass me a note from time to time referring to a drooling parishioner or a wayward child whose parents didn't understand the importance of disciplining their children. Of course, she was more colorful. Sister Lula Mae Moon would join us some Sundays, when she wasn't doing the announcements, singing in the choir, or leading devotion. She and Sister Walker were fun to watch. Sister Moon would often whisper that if Pastor Lewis passed the offering tray one more time during service, "He was gonna look around and come up short." Sister Walker would burst out with a laugh masked by her white handkerchief.

I was excited about becoming involved in a few ministries or maybe even starting a few. I had never desired to be involved in church before. It was a desire I welcomed and was pleased to possess. The church really needed a single's ministry because there was a handful of unmarried twenty and thirty-somethings. I knew I could definitely benefit from one.

"If you are without a church home or maybe a member of a church where you are not being fed the gospel, we now open the doors of the church, inviting you to say 'yes' to Christ and join our church family." The choir started singing "There's Room at the Cross" softly as two ushers put folding chairs at the front of the church facing the pews.

Sister Walker glanced over at me and smiled. She had always expected, or at least hoped I would join, but she never pressured me. I took a deep breath, stood up, grabbed my purse and Bible and walked down the aisle towards the three chairs in front of the pulpit. I smiled as I heard the applause, amens, and the "praise the Lords." I blushed when I saw Pastor Lewis's eyes on me. I took a seat and was quickly approached by Sister Daniels who took down my information.

"Giving all praises to God, the Divine Baptist Church family and Pastor Lewis, today we have Sister Natalie Thomas coming for membership." Sister Daniels said as she spoke to the congregation of about seventy.

Pastor Lewis stepped down from the pulpit and came close enough to me I could smell his very masculine cologne. He put his arm around my shoulder and gave me a gentle pastoral squeeze, a cross between a father's hug and a modest touch.

He took my hand and said to the congregation, "Well, well, well, I have to say, Sister Thomas, it is so nice having you become a part of our church, officially," he joked. "We welcome you to our church family and it is my prayer you will find several ministries to get involved in. Again, welcome."

After church there were several hugs. Sister Walker stayed by my side as to display her new contribution to the ministry. I was pleased when she invited me to help her and Sister Daniels count the money collected during the offering. I had never been invited to do anything like that before and it made me feel special to be trusted enough to be to be partially responsible for something like that.

I followed her up the narrow stairway into a small room adjacent to the room where we held our sorority meetings. Sister Daniels was finishing a phone call with someone who, judging from the language, was a family member.

"How's your niece doing?" Sister Walker asked as she pulled out a hairpin from her purse to secure her long, salt and pepper ringlets into a simple, but elegant chignon.

"She's doing much better, but her fever is not down yet," she said as she looked up and noticed me, "but anyway, let's count this money, cause I have to get out of here and go to Eckerd Drugs to pick up Tamika's prescription."

"You don't have to stay. Go on and tend to your niece. Me and Natalie can take care of this," Sister Walker said as she touched the other woman's shoulder. "Go on now, we've got it," she reassured her.

"Thank you. Tell the pastor, okay?"

"I will, now you go on and get out of here before I change my mind," she smiled at her obviously worried friend and sister in Christ.

My heart went out to Sister Daniels. It was evident the concern for her niece went far beyond the normalcy of an aunt-niece relationship. There was definitely a story there, but I had no idea what it was and it was not my place to inquire.

I could hear Sister Daniel's steps as she walked down the stairs towards the backdoor. The steps came to a stop and I could hear talking. I couldn't make out what was being said, but I did recognize Pastor Lewis's voice.

"Now, look here, Dear, first we separate the checks from the cash. Once that's done we separate the ones, fives, tens, twenties and fifties, etc. You've had jobs where you counted money before, right, Sweetie?"

10

"Actually, no I haven't," I admitted honestly.

"Well, just follow my lead, it's easy." She reassured me as she squeezed my hand and smiled. Sister Walker had a combination of spirituality, style, poise, wisdom, wit and beauty that reminded me of Lena Horne. If I had a living grandmother, I would want her to be just like her.

Less than fifteen minutes later, we were finished counting the money and Sister Walker was showing me how to record the financial logbook. We both glanced towards the doorway when Pastor Lewis appeared.

"How's it going?" he cheerfully said as he entered the room smiling.

"We're just finishing up, Pastor. I was just showing our new member how to record the money," she said, but never looked up from the record book, not wanting to lose her place.

"Good, that's good. You catching on okay, Sister Thomas?" he asked, lightly patting my shoulder.

"Yes, I have a good teacher," I said as I nudged Sister Walker and looked at Pastor Lewis and smiled.

He returned the smile. "Well, how did we do today?"

"Looks like around three thousand, one hundred, forty dollars, and fifty-two cents," Sister Walker reported as she took off the bifocals that had been resting on her pointy nose and made eye contact with Pastor Lewis.

"Not bad, but we slipped a bit from last Sunday, didn't we?" Pastor inquired with a hint of concern in his voice.

"Yeah, but you know how attendance is when it looks like it's going to snow. It keeps people in." Then added, "Oh yes, Sister Daniels had to leave early to check on her niece, did you see her?"

"Yes, I saw her on her way out. Do me a favor and leave a note for Sister Graham to put little Tamika back on the sick and shut in list."

"Will do."

It was definitely interesting to see what goes on behind the pulpit. Amazingly, I had never imagined that the finances of a church would be a major concern of the pastor. I just always took that aspect of the church for granted.

Chapter 3

Over the past few weeks, my little crush on Pastor Lewis had all but disappeared. Yes, he was one of the most handsome men I'd ever seen, but he was also my pastor who was a great teacher and preacher of the Word. Besides, he was at least ten years older and a man I had come to admire and respect. Also, by spending more time in the church office, I speculated that he had a girlfriend. Maybe I was naive, but I had no idea preachers had personal relationships with women. If my instincts were true and they were an item, she didn't look like a woman I felt he would be attracted to. Sister Jackson was 5'2", dark brown skinned, and a big gap between her two front teeth. She definitely wouldn't be considered attractive, but she wasn't ugly either. She did have a way of always smiling, which made her look better. I guess if Pastor Lewis were my man, I'd be smiling, too.

Wednesday night's Bible study was powerful. Pastor Lewis taught on the grace of God. The presence of God was definitely in the church. Every other person was filled by the presence of the Lord by shouting, running and speaking in tongue. I was brought to tears. As Sister Walker put her arm around me for support, I was touched when she handed me her trademark white handkerchief, so I could dry my tears. I realized I had been living much of my life depending on God's grace and mercy. As an account executive, working on commission, I relied on him to grant me wisdom and knowledge on how to deal with customers and the uncertainty of the nature of sales. As a single woman I relied on him to send me a mate, knowing my track record left much to be desired.

After saying goodbye to Sister Walker and a few other sorors that were there, I headed home to prepare for an early morning meeting. The few remaining cars pulled out of the parking lot at the same time I did.

It was a cold winter's night. As I turned onto Lakeshore Drive, I inserted my Juanita Bynum tape on being single and satisfied. I often pulled out my single empowerment tapes when I struggled with the realization I was still single. When I was mapping out my life as a child, I assumed by age twenty-four I would be married and have my first child by twenty-seven. Something drastically went wrong with that plan. I was content with my singlehood, but I often longed for the life I thought I would have had by now.

At the next light, as I was adjusting the volume, I was startled by a honk. As I looked up, I saw Pastor Lewis in his beige Lexus waving at me. Shocked, I returned the wave and quickly looked away. A few seconds later, still feeling his stare, I decided to act as if I was looking in my purse on the passenger's side and sneak a peek. I figured that was a good way to confirm he was still looking without being obvious. He was still looking! After what seemed like minutes, the signal finally turned green and without looking in the direction of his car, I sped off. By the time I turned onto the street that led to my apartment, I checked my rear view mirror and he was not there. What was that all about? Was he just being nice by acknowledging a devoted member or was he flirting? The thought that he might be interested created a flutter of butterflies in my stomach. Even though I was shocked at the fact that I felt that he was flirting, I immediately dismissed it due to the fact there was no way this man who I held in such high regard could possibly be interested in me. He's my pastor, for Christ's sake. I was probably just reading too much into his innocent gesture. But why was he staring, after I had already acknowledged his honk with a wave?

*　*　*

I made it to the office just early enough to reflect on the professional bumpy road I had taken to make it to this day. *Less than six months ago, I walked through the doors as an unfulfilled communications specialist for Lucky Lumber Company. With a growing hatred for writing about the sales of 2x4 and other undesirable building materials, I had to make a change.*

My free time was spent looking through the newspaper for possible career opportunities. An ad expressing a need for a sports marketing representative for a growing marketing company sounded very exciting. I figured since I had a marketing degree, promoting sports in the city known for the best teams in the NBA and NFL would allow me to gain experience in the field, as well as put me in the circle of eligible men. I called in sick at Lucky Lumber and set an appointment for a 9am interview.

Sitting in the lobby of the small building, I wondered if I was in the correct place. This had to be the strangest business setting I'd ever seen. Extremely loud, heavy metal music was blasting, as if to muffle the sounds of yelling and chanting I could faintly hear coming from the rear of the building. The secretary was busy answering the several calls coming in. She answered the phone, "Advertising, how may I help you?" Advertising?? What the hell was advertising? And why didn't she answer the phone stating the name of the company, so I would at least know if I was in the right place? She was pretty vague with the person on the phone when she gave the job description; instead she tried to pressure the person to set an appointment to speak with the manager, so he could address the questions. This was the same spiel she gave to me and apparently a few other applicants waiting because I noticed a few of them making eye contact with one another

The CD, which I think was Led Zeppelin, stopped while the receptionist was on the phone, allowing all of us the opportunity to collect our scattered thoughts. The lack of the loud, hard rock music allowed us the opportunity to clearly hear the shouts, yells, and chanting coming from one of the back rooms of the building. After the phone call, the receptionist quickly rose to her feet to put in another CD. Dressed in her "way too short and thin for winter time," sleeveless mini-dress, she bent down to get a CD out of the case that was positioned under a huge, colorful, psychedelic fish tank. By doing that, two super white, healthy cheeks divided by a pink thong made an unwelcome appearance. That was the last straw for two middle-aged women who walked out in disgust.

Seconds later, a line of eight or ten people walked from the room where all the chants, hoots, and howls originated and went into an office near my seat. I could hear some talking behind the door, but I couldn't make out what was being said. Moments later, a blonde gentleman opened the door and stepped outside the room, holding a clipboard. "Judith Montgomery," he said wearing a smile.

Seated two chairs from me, a woman in her mid-forties collected her briefcase, stood and walked toward the gentleman, who appeared to be the manager. They shook hands and he guided her into the room. A few seconds later, Judith was led out the front door by this barely legal, fuzz-faced kid, with run-over, beat up shoes. Where was she going with him? I knew this interview was to take at least three to four hours, but no one told me anything about going anywhere.

"Natalie Thomas."

I got up and walked toward the room and was introduced to a very obese man in his late twenties to early thirties.

"Natalie Thomas, this is David Lacey. He'll be the most important person you will meet today. It is David's job to evaluate you on your business sense, ability to manage, and your adaptability to different marketing concepts. Have a great day, take a lot of notes, and we will be making our decisions when you make it back."

Off I went, where I didn't know. Mr. Lacey walked me out to the parking lot to his 1995 Pontiac where he explained to me that I would be witnessing the basic, entry-level aspect of the business and he'll explain more as the day progressed. His evasiveness was slightly overshadowed by his kind, non-threatening behavior, so I rolled with the punches and got in his car.

While David was trying his best to make conversation, my mind drifted to the sometimes paranoid warnings my mother has given to me ever since I left home to go to college. Her warnings only intensified when I got in the real world and began living on my own in different states.

"You are just too trusting."
"You are just too naive for your own good."
"You are gonna get yourself killed by being too nice."

She would have a fit if she knew I was in a strange car, with a strange man, going to a strange, unknown place.

16

"Natalie, did you hear me?" David said, interrupting my internal questioning.

"Oh, I'm sorry. What was that?" I responded in an upbeat tone, trying not to let on that I was now worried. Shoot, I didn't bother to write down the license plate number.

"Do you live around here?" He asked, smiling as he reached his fat arm across the front seat, in front of my knees to open his glove compartment and pulled out a pack of Marlboro Light 100's. He then reached in his jacket pocket and pulled out a lighter to ignite the cancer stick, not asking if I cared if he smoked in my presence. He cracked the window allowing some of the smoke to escape.

Okay, now I'm not only unsure of the situation, but he was now pissing me off with his lack of consideration. Hell, the smoking didn't bother me because my dad smoked while I was growing up, so I was used to the smell, but he didn't know that and didn't have the consideration to ask. He should be asking about my goals, work history, and career motivations.

"I'm not too far from the office." Wanting to get back to the subject at hand, I then added, "Where exactly are we going?"

"We are actually approaching it in about another couple of exits, you'll see." Again, with the evasiveness.

Just when I was about to ask him to take me back to the office, we were in Vernon Hills, a small town outside of Chicago. After the car was parked, David got out of the car and headed towards the trunk. Confused, I followed to keep up and to see what was really going on. As he opened his truck, I saw a huge box of pagers. David reached in and handed me four pagers and he took five or six and positioned them under his fat arm. He closed the trunk and we began to walk towards this strip mall across the street.

"So, what are we doing with these?" I asked trying to keep up. I was amazed that he could walk so fast.

17

"You are going to see the direct marketing aspect of the business," he responded.

"This is a sales job?" I asked disappointedly.

"You will see the direct marketing today. When you return to the office later on, the manager will explain all aspects of the business, okay?"

I felt suckered. No wonder they were so evasive. Part of me wanted to leave, but the intrigue of seeing this man in action made we want to stay. Plus, I had already taken the day off, so I might as well try and make the best of it.

As we entered the travel agency and approached an agent in her mid-twenties, I listened to David say, "Hello, I'm David and this is Natalie and we are from Metrophone Paging Company. We are doing a promotion today by giving out free pagers."

"Free pagers?" The agent said as she raised her head, displaying interest in what she just heard.

"Yes, absolutely free pagers, check it out." With much bravado, David places the pager in her hand for a few seconds then takes it back. "The pager is free and all you have to do is use the service."

"Well, how much is the service?" She inquired looking interested.

"We have different plans, let me show you."

In the next twenty minutes, the happy young lady signed a contract for service for not one, but two pagers and before we could exit the store another associate who was listening two desks away asked to sign up for a free pager with the service.

The rest of the day was filled with a lot of the same. From what I could determine, David made at least four other sales during the next two to three hours we were out there. We walked in almost every kind of business from used car places to beauty salons. All in all, it was a good day, with good company, but I had questions.

Sitting across the table from Harry Bell, I was impressed as he broke down the business and explained that if I could learn to promote and sell the products well enough to teach it to others, I could move into management within an eight to nine month period. He explained how the company planned to branch off to New York, Minnesota and Florida within the year and he was looking for people who could not only sell, but could teach the aspects of selling and promotions to other people in the new markets as they became available.

This was great, I knew I could do what I saw David do, and probably do it better and faster. It was new to me, but I wanted something new and exciting.

"Do you have any questions so far?" Harry asked.

The compensation had not been brought up yet. It was not proper interview etiquette for me to ask, at least not yet.

"No, this sounds great, continue please," I said with a smile.

"Okay, great. Now here's our commission schedule." Harry opened his desk and pulled out a laminated presentation card.

My heart dropped. Commission, no, it can't be.

"How many pagers did you see David sell today?"

"I think it was six or seven."

"Well, as you can see," as he pointed to the card with the figures on it, "David made about one hundred and eighty five dollars today. Granted he had a short day because he was interviewing and he had to return to the office a little earlier than the standard eight hour work day, but he had a profitable day."

There was silence. *"So, let me make sure I understand, he made one hundred and eighty five dollars plus his salary?"* I asked with dollar signs in my eyes.

"No, David made one hundred and eighty five dollars. In the initial phases in our business there is no salary, but as a manager you are guaranteed a base of at least sixty thousand plus bonuses."

My mind was spinning a mile a minute. I sat and pondered for what seemed to be thirty minutes. I had never worked on commission before. I thought about my rent, car note, utilities and insurance. Could I do this long enough to reach a management level and not go broke? I slowly broke down my current annual salary as a communication specialist of twenty-seven thousand — per month and then per day. After the calculations, I was making approximately one hundred dollars a day. Being self-motivated, I knew I could do anything I put my mind to. Then it occurred to me, why put in one hundred percent of my energy for someone else and make a hundred dollars a day, when I could put in that same one hundred percent and make more than one hundred and fifty dollars with the opportunity to make more in time.

"If given the opportunity, do you think you can reach a management position within a year by doing exactly what you saw David do today?" Harry asked. *"Can you see yourself managing an office?"* He reclined in his chair, while never breaking eye contact.

"I know I can do what I saw David do today and to be perfectly honest, Harry, I would have to make it to a management level in less than six months, not a year." I added, *"Management is the only reason why I would consider the job. The sales part is okay, but I look at it as a means to an end. If offered the position, I would accept only with that ultimate goal in mind."*

"You sound like the motivated person we've been looking for. On behalf of everyone at Import Sales Incorporated, we'd like you to be a part of our team." Harry said with a huge smile and extended his hand.

I smiled, accepted his handshake and never looked back.

Chapter 4

"I would like to take the opportunity to present to you the newest member of our management team. Natalie has taken a nine to twelve month management-training program average and accomplished it in only six months. There are fourteen people in this room she has personally trained, each one profiting over eight hundred dollars a week. This is a standard we are excited to spread in new markets and there's no one more qualified to do it than her. Everyone give a huge round of applause to Natalie Thomas, our newest manager," Harry said.

As I took the podium, I did something that was totally unexpected. I cried. While Harry was talking I reflected on the lessons learned while I was with the company. Never having worked on commission before, I learned the true meaning of self-motivation and hard work ethic. There were many days I would come home exhausted and days I questioned if it was all worth it. There were countless days I ate fried salami sandwiches for dinner and rolled pennies for gas money, but I was determined not to quit. I was also proud that I did it on my own, with no financial assistance from my parents. They had no idea I was doing direct sales; if they had they would have worried to death. This whole experience made me realize I had more within myself than I ever thought I had.

"I would like to thank Harry and the other managers for allowing me the opportunity to become a part of this wonderful team. To all the people I had an opportunity to train, I learned just as much from you as you learned from me. Everyone in this room can accomplish whatever you want if you believe in yourself and never give up. I'm not going to say it won't be hard. I had a many of days when I wanted to quit because the road got a little too hard, but that's when you try that much harder. I appreciate you all, and thank you for everything," I concluded as I wiped a lingering tear, not knowing what else to say.

After the meeting I stood in the lobby shaking hands and hugging everyone. This was the first day I did not have to go into the field to sell, but instead, I could stay in the office and learn all the inner-office stuff. This would be the day I had dreamed of.

"How are you doing?" Harry asked, smiling as he motioned for me to come in his office and take a seat.

"Great, it's been an awesome morning and I'm looking forward to knowing what you guys do during the day while I'm out in the field," I said jokingly.

"We'll definitely get to that. I'm so proud of your accomplishments with us, Natalie," he paused. "Just so you are aware, we just obtained a huge client. This client has the potential to generate triple the revenue of our present clientele. I'm interested to know, how do you feel about the Big Apple?"

"I've never been, but I've always wanted to visit," I said enthusiastically, figuring he may want me to manage a road trip or a test market for a week or two.

"Good, because in two weeks the company's opening an office in Ronkonkoma, New York and we want you to manage it."

Was I hearing correctly? Did he just say he wanted me to move to New York and manage a location? Not knowing how to react, but realizing that relocation was always part of their plan for me, I said, "New York, great, give me the details."

Chapter 5

The next month was like a giant cyclone. I packed all my belongings, moved to New York with six guys who believed in me enough to relocate and put their careers in my hands. My opening date was the first week of January. Everything happened so fast, I didn't even tell my friends, sorors, or church family I was moving. Instead, I chose to send everyone a Christmas card with a little note apologizing for my abrupt move and explaining my new venture. I included my cell and home number in the Christmas card to my church and Sister Walker, just in case anyone wanted to keep in touch. After all, Sister Walker and Pastor Lewis had become important people in my life and contributed a great deal to my spiritual growth and happiness while living in Chicago.

I chose to travel home to Dallas, Texas for the holidays to visit my friends and family. Exiting the plane, the airport was filled with people, but I was looking for my daddy. I knew he was hiding somewhere. He always positioned himself where he could see me, but I could not see him. I think he got a kick out of seeing me look for him. After walking past all of the smiling faces of people waiting to greet their loved ones, I saw mine. As I ran up to him, I felt like his little girl. He looked so handsome. I was so relieved because the last time I had visited he had lost a lot of weight due to an irreversible heart condition. Apparently his medication was working, because I saw no signs of sickness. We embraced for a few seconds; he took my luggage and walked to the car.

An hour later, I was home. Entering the house I grew up in, all of my senses told me this house was home. The living room looked the same. It had the same floral printed furniture and the same framed photographs that froze time of the little girl that now returned as a woman. There was that same clean, crisp smell that told me my mother had done a thorough job with the lemon scented Pinesol, bleach and furniture polish. I could hear *Merry Christmas, Baby* playing on the radio. The feeling was welcoming and familiar.

Christmas day started off wonderfully. My mom, dad, sister, brother-in-law, godparents, and my three best friends shared a huge meal. There wasn't much left of the turnip greens, hen, dressing, brisket, chitterlings, baked macaroni and cheese, hot water cornbread, candied yams, black-eyed peas, seven up cake, and peach cobbler after everyone had their first, seconds and thirds.

After the meal, we all retired to the warm, cozy, living room and listened to festive Christmas tunes while we exchanged gifts. Later, we watched holiday classics like *Imitation of Life* and *It's a Wonderful Life*. My dad got a lively game of spades and dominoes going, which he won. A couple of hours later, my friends and I decided to go to the movies to see the opening of *Titanic*.

Cindy, Sandy, and Toni were three of my best friends. We met in high school and stayed very close throughout the years. As I got into Sandy's red Jeep Cherokee, I put in *The Miseducation of Lauren Hill*. This was Cindy's Christmas present to me. In turn, I had gotten each one of them the book *The Color Complex*. It was the best book I had read that year and one I thought each one would find enlightening. The book focused on the politics of skin color between the Black race and how White America perceives Blacks of different shades. I always gave gifts that I had a special connection with, so the person not only could benefit from it by becoming more self-aware or intellectually stimulated, but also be touched, as I was touched. Each one of us had unique experiences in dealing with skin color that had shaped our self-image and ultimately our lives. Cindy and Sandy were caramel colored identical twins who stood five feet nine and were voted "most beautiful" in high school. Toni was yellow-boned, five feet six, very slender and very cute. I was somewhere in between, standing five feet seven and 135 pounds, cinnamon brown in color with dimples. People always commented that we could all pass for sisters, even now, despite the difference in our color.

All of our social lives started out pretty slow. Mine was the slowest. I didn't date much in school for the obvious reasons for that time. My type was not "in". If you weren't light skinned with long hair and a cute curvacious shape, you weren't too popular with the guys. I had none of that. I grew up knowing I wasn't necessarily

24

considered pretty, but I wasn't ugly either. Luckily, I got more attractive with age. That's another reason why I tried so hard to look my best now because I grew up trying to make the best of what God had given me. So, I'll spend a few extra minutes in the mirror with my hair and makeup or I'll invest a little more money in my wardrobe. Amazingly, with all the looks and compliments I receive as an adult, in my mind I was that little girl that just didn't quite measure up. Looking back, I guess it was a blessing I didn't grow up thinking I was cute because I excelled in all other areas to compensate.

After the movie, we were hyped. We couldn't help but dissect the tragedy of the story versus the love story in the plot. We were amazed by the jaw-dropping special effects and we all debated whether or not we thought Leonardo DiCaprio was cute. When I was about to give my two cents, my cell phone rang and interrupted our lively conversation.

"Hello?"

"Sister Thomas, hi, this is Pastor Lewis." My heart stopped. What was he doing calling me?

"Oh, my God, hi, Pastor Lewis."

"I was just calling to tell you Merry Christmas and that I received your Christmas card. So, you're in New York now?"

"Well, yes, my company moved me to New York, but now I'm in Dallas visiting my family for the Holiday," I replied.

"We are definitely going to miss you. I know you are probably with family now, so I'm not going to hold you, but I'm going to be in New York in a week and I wanted to see if I could visit with you?"

My brain was working overtime. I couldn't believe what I was hearing. Before I could let what he asked me settle in my mind I said, "Okay, that would be great. Just call me a few days before you come, so I can make arrangements."

"I definitely will. Talk to you soon and have a Merry Christmas."

"You, too. Bye." I said as I pressed end on my cell phone.

"Who was that?" Sandy asked.

I couldn't dare tell her the truth. How could I be honest with her and explain a situation I couldn't explain or understand myself? I admit I had been attracted to Pastor Lewis, but my crush was long gone and had been for months. Yes, he was very attractive, articulate, and educated, but he was my pastor and I had started seeing him in that light.

"That was a friend of mine from Chicago and they're planning a trip to visit me in New York," I answered. If it were only that simple.

* * *

"Natalie, breakfast is ready," my mom knocked then opened the door to announce.

I raised my head to look at the digital clock to see that it was 7:15. Jesus. I had almost forgotten the fact that there's no sleeping late in the Thomas household. I was in a house full of early birds. Maybe because both of my parents were raised in the country and used to getting up with the chickens, they always woke up at the crack of dawn and expected everyone to follow suit.

There was nothing like breakfast at home. I had often deprived myself of the "most important meal of the day" due to lack of time with my busy schedule. Walking into the kitchen, my mom and dad were fixing their plates with fried eggs, homemade hash browns, cream of wheat and ham. It smelled good and tasted better. They took the time during breakfast to ask me about my relocation and if I would miss my friends in Chicago. I told them I was extremely excited about the new challenges I was faced with, but a little scared at the same time. This was a big step for me. I was going to be the first African-American area manager in the company's history. Not to mention I was one of only a handful of women who had made it to that level. They both gave me words of encouragement and said how proud they were of me and if I needed anything to just call. This made me feel good because it was important to me to make my parents proud and to know they supported me.

I always tried really hard to impress them, mainly because I grew up in the shadow of a sister who had done just that. Making good grades, excelling in sports and having a successful career always came easy for her. Every achievement, whether it was grades, a pageant win, scholarships or career accomplishments came with blood, sweat and tears for me.

The drive to the airport saddened me. I had a really nice stay that unfortunately had to come to an end. I was satisfied to see that my mom and dad were getting along great and my dad's health seemed to be okay. I just wished I could have spent more time.

"Delta Airlines Flight 222 would like to welcome all first class passengers to board the aircraft," the female attendant announced in a cheerful voice.

My mother stood up and Daddy followed.

"Well, Natalie, I guess we are gonna go now. You take care." My mother said and gave me a quick hug.

My dad then stepped to embrace me in a long tight hug and said in my ear, "You call us when you make it in, hear?" His voice cracked with emotion.

"I sure will. I had a good time." I wanted to say more. I needed to tell them I loved them. Those were words I had never said to them, nor ever heard myself, but it was known.

Disappointed in myself for not being able to express myself verbally, I grabbed my carry on and looked back to see them walk away.

Chapter Six

The next few days were hectic in New York. I was trying to learn my way around the city and its five boroughs. My days were divided by doing interviews in the morning and going in the field to assure myself that the guys who moved with me were solid enough to train the new starts. Although the new promotion was simple and an easy moneymaker, I wanted the guys' average to be to where they were profiting at least two hundred dollars a day. We were not in Chicago any more, so the veteran agents had to show the new starts how to sell enough to make a living in a city where the cost of living was one of the highest in the nation.

By mid-week the office had exploded from seven to twenty-two. This was a huge accomplishment, but one that didn't come easy. I was exhausted and my senior distributors were, too. We were working fourteen-hour days, but things were coming together. Everyone was determined to bring the office to thirty people by next week. I didn't want an office with a lot of weak people in sales. Growth had to be done with strength. Training had to be top of the line. It could be done, but only with one hundred percent dedication from everyone. We were going to be the number one office.

* * *

Thursday night, I walked in my apartment and collapsed on my couch. Exhausted, I opened my eyes to see the red button blinking on my voice mail to indicate I had messages. Taking off my heels as I walked towards my phone, I picked up the receiver and heard the automated voice say, "You have three new messages."

The first message was from my daddy.

"Heeeyy, Nat, I was just calling to see how you're doing up there. Give me a call when you get the message, no hurry." I smiled. I could picture my dad's face sporting a huge grin. He had the type of voice that smiled over the phone.

28

The second message was from Sister Walker.

"Sweetie, it's Sister Walker. I can't believe you left me without saying goodbye. Call me." I felt bad about not saying goodbye. I had to call her.

The third message was short and simple.

"Sister Thomas, this is Pastor Lewis. There's been a change in plans. I'll be in New York in two weeks. I have to do a funeral this weekend. I don't know if you remember Sister Ray. She passed away in Mississippi and I'm conducting her funeral on Saturday. Call me at home when you get the message. My number is 708-555-4457."

I hung up the phone feeling confused and relieved. Although, I did not know Sister Ray, I was glad her passing took place to avoid an encounter I still questioned. I was tired of questioning Pastor Lewis's intentions and decided to find out what his intentions were. The two-week delay was good because I did not need any distractions during the start of my new office, plus I needed time to figure out his intentions.

I called home first. My family was back to its regular routine following the holiday. My mom seemed to be in a good mood. She was telling me that a lady at her church had on a dress so tight that the deacons couldn't pray straight without cutting their eyes at her during devotion. My mom loved that kind of stuff. She then told me she sent me a care package with some "goodies" she knew I would like. My mother always made sure that my needs were taken care of. Her care packages normally included books, nonperishable foods, a card, and at least a twenty-dollar bill. She knew I probably did not need anything, but if I did, I would never ask, so to give her peace of mind she sent me a package at least once a month. My mother demonstrated her love to others by gift giving. I loved her for that. I then heard some coughing in the background.

"Is that Daddy?" I asked.

"Yeah, he's fighting a cold. Hold on — he wanted to speak to you."

"Heeeyyy, Nat, what going on?"

"Nothing much, just trying to stay warm, it's supposed to snow later on. How are you doing? Momma said you're fighting a little cold."

I always worried about my dad. When I was in college, he had a mild heart attack. He recovered nicely, but he went through a phase where he was hospitalized and lost a lot of weight. Due to his heart attack, doctors advised that unnecessary stress and negativity had to be eliminated, so I checked on him weekly.

He told me that he had a tickle in his throat, but it wasn't a cold. It was just like him to belittle anything related to his health. He did not want anyone to worry about him. He asked me how my car was holding up and if I had gotten the oil changed. He seemed at ease when I told him I had gotten my oil changed when I made it back from my visit to Dallas. I could feel his excitement over the phone when I told him about the growth of the office and our company goals for this month. He mentioned how proud he was of me and that he and momma were going to plan a visit, once I was settled.

My next call was to Sister Walker. Disappointed, I got her answering machine. "You've reached the Walker residence. At this time no one is available to answer your call. Please leave a message and may God bless you." Her voice was filled with aged wisdom and sweetness.

"Sister Walker, it's Natalie Thomas, I got your message. I'm so sorry I haven't called you. I'm doing fine and I'll call you later. Tell everyone I said hello," I said and then hung up the phone.

I walked into my bedroom and started to undress. I needed a moment to myself to reflect before I called Pastor Lewis. As I sat on the edge of my bed, I envisioned what the conversation would reveal. Needing relaxation, I walked into the bathroom and ran water for my bath. Running my fingers underneath the water to test the temperature, I grabbed my scented rock salt my sister made for me as a Christmas gift and sprinkled it in the tub. I stood up and walked over to my collection of scented candles, where I chose Jasmine and lit the wick with my cigarette lighter.

I stood in my black bra and panties and looked at myself in the mirror. Months of doing outside sales had toned my legs to the point of where I had definition. Busy days with long hours had flattened my stomach because my schedule was so busy I didn't eat breakfast and barely had lunch.

I walked into the bedroom and put in my newest Maxwell CD. There was something about his voice that put me in a state of longing, relaxation and hopefulness, all at the same time. As the lyrics from *This Woman's Work* started to play, I walked back into the bathroom, cut off the lights and the water. I took off my lace panties and stepped in the tub. The heat of the tub was just hot enough. Perfect. As I lowered my body into the tub, I closed my eyes and let out a sigh releasing the pressures from the day.

I must have fallen asleep in the tub because the sound of my phone startled me. I jumped out of the tub, reached for my towel, and ran to the phone resting on my bedroom nightstand. I answered the phone so fast I didn't even check my caller-id.

"Hello?"

"Sister Thomas, this is Pastor Lewis."

"Pastor Lewis, hi, how are you?" I responded, amazingly calm. My heart was palpitating a mile per second. Breathe. Remain calm.

"I'm blessed. Did you get my message?" He asked with his voice sounding smoother and more relaxed than the message he left earlier on my voice mail.

"Yes, I did. I just got home a few minutes ago," I said.

"Well, my visit has been delayed due to a few things popping up and Sister Ray's funeral this weekend. Did you ever meet Sister Ray?" he casually asked.

"No, I was trying to remember her face after listening to your message."

"She was one of the founding members of the church. She's the sister of Sister Lula Mae Moon. She was a sweet lady. She had a long battle with breast cancer. But listen, I didn't mean to disturb you. I just wanted to let you know I'd be flying in on January twenty-second. That's on a Thursday. Will you be able to pick me up from the airport?" He quickly asked as if to not give me a chance to think about what he just asked.

"Sure," I answered reluctantly. "Are you preaching at a church in New York that weekend?" I figured this question would let me know how long he planned on staying and also the actual motive for the trip.

"I do have some old college buddies in Harlem I'd like to contact, but I just really want to visit you,'" he said in a serious, yet non-threatening tone.

"Okay, yeah, I don't mind. Just call me with your flight information a few days before hand, so I can make arrangements for the office to be covered," I said.

"Thanks. Well, Sister Thomas, I'll be in contact and I look forward to seeing you in a couple of weeks. I have to counsel a couple in a minute, but it was really nice talking to you."

Not knowing exactly how to end the call I simply said, "Goodnight, Pastor Lewis, talk to you soon."

It only took a second after I ended the phone call to realize that my instinct had been correct. Pastor Lewis was interested. Even though the tone of his voice remained friendly and professional and didn't imply a romantic interest, his words revealed his motives were to spend time with me. I did not want to over analyze the conversation or make it into something that it wasn't, but my spirit was telling me there's more to his visit than he was letting me know. Regardless, I was now suddenly anticipating his arrival like a child counting down to Christmas.

I spent the remainder of the night tossing and turning. I just couldn't relax enough to fall asleep without thinking about Pastor Lewis. The thought that the man I had once admired from afar was coming to see me gave me goose bumps. The fact that we weren't close friends and never worked closely enough in the ministry for us to have developed a close working relationship led me to believe he saw something in me that he wanted to explore. The thought made me smile, but also made me leery. It's not like he was just a fine guy I knew in Chicago; he was my pastor and I wasn't sure how I should feel about that.

* * *

The next two weeks flew by. My office had expanded to over thirty-one professional people. I had also hired a secretary that was costing me more than the average office, but I was not going to have a Hustler pin-up represent my company. After all, the first person my prospective contractors heard and saw when they walked in the door to inquire about a job was her. She not only represented my company, but she was also a direct reflection of me and the caliber of people I wanted in my office.

I was paying Janet Brooks five hundred dollars a week, plus lunches, and so far she was worth it. She was beautiful. She was 5'7" with a slender build. She had very fair skin with long sandy hair. Her physical beauty was complemented with a gorgeous smile and warm, welcoming voice. She was a HBCU graduate of Morris Brown College with a degree in Business Administration. It was important for my secretary to be pleasing to the eyes, educated, motivated, and assertive. The primary reason she accepted the job is for the growth potential I explained during the interview. It was my goal to train her to conduct the interviews and some minimal evaluations and she would be compensated accordingly. For now, she was just learning the ropes.

"Natalie, you have a call on line two," she stuck her head in the door and said.

"Did you find out who it was?" I asked as I looked up from my sales report from last week.

"Oh, yes, I'm sorry. It's Pastor Lewis," she answered as she read the name off of her note pad and then returned to her desk to answer the phones.

I looked at my calendar and realized it was Tuesday. Oh, my God, he was scheduled to arrive in two days! Even though I had anticipated the arrival, I wasn't consumed with it. I had enough to keep me busy between my conference calls, sales meetings and interviews. The time flew by without my noticing. All of a sudden I was warm all over. As I prepared to answer, I had to concentrate on getting it together. I closed my eyes and took a deep breath — inhale, now exhale. I stared at the blinking red light on the phone, realizing he was just on the other end of the line, I took another deep breath, regained my composure and slowly picked up the phone and pressed line two.

"This is Ms. Thomas, how may I help you?" I asked in my most sexy, yet professional voice, trying to appear as though I didn't know who was on the other end.

"Sister Thomas, this is Pastor Lewis, how are you?" he asked in a very casual, yet friendly tone.

"Good, how are you doing?" My tongue stopped me from saying more.

"I'm doing fine, I was just calling to tell you I'll be arriving at JFK at 2:20 on Thursday afternoon."

"Okay, do you have a flight number?" I asked as I clumsily looked for my pen, knocking over my glass of water. The contracts would have to be retyped.

"Yes, it's going to be flight 736 flying from O'Hare on Continental Airlines," he answered." What is the weather like there?"

"It's been in the forties for the past few days, so bring a coat." I responded with nervous energy. Something within myself would not allow the questions to come from my lips that I really needed to know the answers to. I didn't want to do or say anything to turn him off. My respect for his role as a pastor and my attraction to him made me feel insecure.

"Okay, I have to go conduct Power Prayer Lunch that starts in another fifteen minutes, so I'll see you then. Thanks again and I'm looking forward to spending some time with you," he said in a hurried tone.

"Bye, Bye. See you then." Lord have mercy.

Chapter Seven

The next day, I took a few hours off and ran some errands to prepare for Pastor Lewis's arrival. I went to the mall and picked up a really cute burgundy suit. It was a tailored look that complemented my figure and complexion. I then stopped by Super Wal-mart and purchased some catfish fillets, hollandaise sauce, coffee, wild rice, paper towels, mouthwash, carpet freshener, bleach, and Febreeze. Since it was still unclear on whether or not he was staying with me, I had to be prepared with everything I thought I would need.

I made it home later than I hoped, due to several final interviews I had to conduct. Walking into my one bedroom, I disrobed, put on my faded Delta Sigma Theta sweats and started cleaning. Two hours later, after vacuuming, mopping, dusting, dishes and washing of two loads of clothes, I looked across my twelve hundred feet of living space and smiled. My apartment was spotless and smelled crispy-clean. I was ready for the unknown.

That night I tossed and turned. My anxious energy was almost overwhelming. I kept thinking about what the next day held. Regardless of what it had in store for me, I was eagerly anticipating it. My feelings varied from nervousness to great desire. My nervousness derived from the uncertainty of his motives, what the next few days would reveal and my own feelings. My desire was to have a man I greatly admired to admire me in return. That's all I ever wanted in a mate. I wanted my bland existence of singlehood to be filled with a man who adored me with all of his soul. Maybe he was that man. From what I had seen, he could be.

Beams of light shining through my bedroom window pried my eyes open before my alarm sounded. As I got out of my bed, I stretched and looked out of my window to find the makings of a majestic day. The sky was the ocean with wisps of clouds defining waves; the sun splashed and bled its brightness across the blue. I quickly made my bed, brushed my teeth, showered and put on a black sweater and black slacks, accessorized by a gold belt.

I went into the office an hour early to plan my morning meeting and to get things organized enough to run in my absence. I was leaving the office around ten o'clock and wasn't returning until the morning. I had instructed Janet not to schedule any interviews for the day and to call me on my cell phone if there was a situation she could not handle.

By 11am I had returned home to prepare for my much-anticipated guest. I laid out my new burgundy suit, accessories and my black leather boots. I took another quick shower with my Victoria Secrets pear scented shower gel. After my shower, I lotioned my body, put on my burgundy tights, suit and boots, and I carefully applied my makeup, making sure that my MAC foundation was evenly distributed. I chose a light gloss for my lips with a hint of deep red undertones. I put a few fresh curls in my hair and shaped my locks with my hands positioning some of it to hang over my shoulders. I reached for my Paloma Picasso perfume and sprayed behind my ears, on my wrist, and on my suit jacket. I then looked at myself in my full mirror. I looked pretty and smelled delectable. I had never seen myself as the image looking back at me, but I liked her. I just hoped Pastor Lewis would, too.

I looked at the clock and saw that it was almost one o'clock. I had to run because I had a forty-five minute commute to JFK. I grabbed my black leather purse and walked out the door, not knowing whether the next time I crossed the threshold would be with Pastor Lewis.

As I turned into the parking lot of JFK my stomach was a web of knots with butterflies trapped and fluttering. There was an accident on the freeway that produced a major traffic jam. Where I had thought I would have about thirty minutes to gain my composure and freshen up in the airport while I waited for Pastor Lewis's plane, it turned out I would only have ten minutes. I parked my Mazda in the overcrowded parking lot and walked briskly to the automatic doorway leading into the Continental terminal.

I looked at the screen that had the arrival and departure times. His flight was on time and was arriving two gates away. Walking to gate seventeen, I stopped in the ladies room and checked my look. Everything was still in place except my insides. I took a few deep

37

breaths to gain my composure, then checked my purse and found a peppermint to freshen my breath. I walked to the gate where people were seated. I wondered if they were as knotted up as I was? Showtime was only three minutes away.

I looked towards the huge window and saw a few mothers holding small children who were pointing in amazement at the huge plane creeping across the expansive tarmac pulling up to the gate.

"Continental Airlines now welcomes Flight 736 from Chicago O'Hare to gate seventeen," the petite agent said.

I slowly made my way to the door that was soon to open for several business people, husbands, wives, relatives, and friends and a man I wasn't sure how to classify The passengers started to deplane, spaced at first, and then more and more grouped in clusters as they exited the terminal. Through all the people coming from the plane, I saw a head that stood taller than most walking toward the exit of the terminal. It was him.

I stood, not knowing how to stand. My lips half curved, not knowing how I should be smiling. I hoped, not knowing what to hope for.

He was wearing a navy blue suit, white shirt, no tie. The first two buttons on his shirt were unbuttoned exposing a chocolate brown collarbone and a few chest hairs. He was relaxed and at ease, carrying his coat in one hand and a garment bag in the other. He saw me and returned my smile with a broad boyish grin, exposing a set of teeth so white and straight I felt a desire to kiss him. I immediately felt guilty.

As we briskly approached each other, I was taken off guard by the quick, tight, half body hug. I hate those hugs because they seem so impersonal. Afterwards, we just stood there looking at each other and smiling for what seemed to be ten seconds. It was awkward. I didn't know what to say and without his motives being defined, I didn't know how to act. All I knew was that he looked handsome and his smile warmed my heart, yet it made me uneasy without knowing the reasons behind the smile.

My nerves teetered precariously from being shot to cracking in two during the uncomfortable moment which, for my sake, had to end. "So, how was your flight?"

"The flight was good. It's nice to see you. You look really nice."

I wanted to tell him he looked better than I remembered. I wanted to tell him that he smelled really good. Most of all, I wanted to tell him that his visit was like a dream come true. Instead I chose a subtle approach, "It's nice seeing you, too. How did you leave Chicago?"

"The church is doing good. We have about one hundred members on the books; about seventy-five of those are active. Things are going well. Sister Walker is really missing your help counting the money," he added jokingly.

"Do you have any more luggage?"

"Nope. This is it," he answered as he slightly raised his bag. "I've learned in all of my travels the necessities for the road."

The automatic door opened and the forty plus degrees hit both of us in the face. Pastor Lewis paused just long enough to put on his coat in one effortless motion. I took the lead as we scurried across the busy street to the parking garage.

I unlocked the door from the driver's side and slid in. Feeling unsure of the effect all that wind had on my hair, I quickly swept my hair behind my ear on the side where he would be sitting, before he had an opportunity to get in the car and notice my swift primping act.

When he got in the car and closed the door, he reached in the pocket of his coat and pulled out his cell phone. "I need to call the church and check in."

I put my stick shift in reverse and accidentally touched his long leg. *Shoot, I hope he knows I didn't do that purposely.* He looked a little uncomfortable in my small car, but didn't say anything.

I was on pins and needles; I could swear my face was shining from perspiration, despite the temperature. Thoughts about the next two hours, hell, the next twenty-four hours were running through my mind. I didn't even know where I was suppose to be taking him. Before I knew it, I was at the booth to pay the fee for parking. I turned to look in the back seat for my purse to retrieve money for the toll. There was a dollar bill in his hand. I gave the attendant the money, but was more focused on the conversation Pastor Lewis was having on the phone.

"Well, call Sister Grimes about the deaconess meeting, she was appointed to take care of it. Tell her if she has any questions to call me on my cell phone, not at home, she knows I'm traveling, but you know she's kind of absent-minded at times," he said jokingly. He then burst out in laughter, as if the person on the other line had agreed and added their own two cents.

Hearing him joke around and laugh like that showed a more human side to him that I didn't know he had. I didn't know preachers had that side to their personality. I guess if all you see is the "preacher" you can easily lose sight of the man.

"Excuse me, Pastor, but where are we going?" I interrupted his call with a nudge.

"Janice, hold on for a second," he told the lady on the other end of the line. "I'm so sorry. I'm hungry? Are you hungry?" he said while placing his hand on his stomach.

"Yeah, I am, now that you mention it," I said smiling nervously at him.

"I can eat anything. Where ever you want to eat is fine," he returned to his conversation. His tone was the same relaxed, friendly tone it had been since he landed. This eased my nerves a bit, but I couldn't help but to wonder if that was all there was to his visit.

During the drive several questions kept popping in my head. I wondered if he was as nervous as I was, or does he make visits to all of his attractive female members? If he were planning to stay with me, where would he sleep? I had a one bedroom apartment and if he thought he was gonna get some, he'd better think again. I was definitely attracted to him, but there was no way I was going there with any man this soon, especially not my pastor. I decided to dismiss that thought because he wasn't giving me any sexual vibes and he was a man of the cloth, so that shouldn't even be an issue.

The next thirty minutes were filled with Pastor Lewis catching me up with different members I knew when I attended his church. From the time we got on the freeway until we pulled into the parking lot of Zappito's Italian Cuisine, he filled me in on the "caliber" of new members that have joined the church. He seemed to be proud of the fact that eighty percent of the church were educators, attorneys, doctors, or corporate executives. I thought to myself what difference did it make what their professions were, but I didn't question. I'm sure he had his reasons.

After parking the car, we walked casually to the restaurant. I felt an arm on the small of my back guiding me up the stairway to the entryway and the nausea returned, but I had to admit it felt good to experience this subtle, yet caring gesture. He opened the door, allowing me to walk in first.

The atmosphere of the restaurant was very romantic. The lighting was dim and the white tablecloths served as the resting place of a single red rose in a beautiful vase on the center of every table surrounded by individual rose pedals. Music from what seemed to be an Italian opera gave the room a feel of romance Italy is known for. Looking at the few couples seated around the restaurant holding hands and looking into each other's eyes, I wish I had made another selection. I didn't want to give Pastor Lewis the wrong impression. I had heard this restaurant had the best Italian food in town, but I had never dined there before.

"Is this okay?" I shyly asked, not knowing what he might be thinking of the atmosphere.

"This is great. It smells good."

The waiter sat us at a table near a window with a view of the wonderful Manhattan skyline. "Since I have been in New York, I have been too busy to appreciate the beauty of the city," I said with my eyes fixed on the magnificent buildings.

"This is one of my favorite cities in the world." He reached across the table and put his hand on mine, caressed it, then removed it and turned his attention back to the view.

I felt like I was going to faint. I actually got lightheaded. Why was he making physical contact with me? I had to excuse myself to gain my composure. I was overwhelmed with the romantic atmosphere, the latest demonstration of closeness, the hopes, and the fact I needed to pee something awful because of nerves. I knew if I excused myself to the ladies' room he would be watching me. The thought of it made me feel like a little girl, but I had to go.

"Excuse me, I need to go the ladies room," I said while standing.

"Okay, hurry back," he said in a deep seductive voice I wasn't ready for.

I scanned and then spotted the ladies room on the other end of the restaurant directly in front of the direction Pastor Lewis was seated. Shit, he had the perfect seat to watch me. This made me feel so uncomfortable. Taking a deep breath, I made every attempt to display my cutest walk as I made my way to my destination maneuvering my way past the tables, couples, and waiters carrying massive trays of cuisine trying desperately not to make contact with any of them.

Relieved that I finally made it to the restroom, I went over to the sink, placed my hands on the counter, closed my eyes, hung my head and exhaled. As I raised my head, I looked at my reflection in the mirror. Shoot, I needed to freshen my makeup. I had an unattractive shine. After reapplying the necessities and taming my hair, I smiled, realizing the man I had long admired was right outside the doors, seated a few feet away waiting for my return.

Walking towards the table, I noticed Pastor Lewis had on glasses and was looking over the menu. The reading glasses gave him a distinguished look that amazingly made him even more attractive, something I thought was impossible. Half way to the table he noticed me and smiled.

As I took my seat, he was still staring at me. I could feel blood rush to may face.

"You are luminous," he said looking like he meant every syllable.

"Luminous?" not knowing how to respond.

"Totally. You stand out in a crowd of people and you are gorgeous."

I was sure I was blushing. "Well, thank you. I appreciate it." I turned my attention to the menu.

Dinner was great. Pastor Lewis told me about his father dying of cancer five years ago. The sickness was the cause of him relocating from Denver to Chicago and attaining an associate pastor position of a small baptist church and a job as a customer service representative for an insurance company, while caring for his dad. After two years, God gave him a vision for a church and he kissed his "dead end job" goodbye. Sadly, later on that year, his dad died.

He was extremely interested in my office. When I told him about the growth of the team, he was very impressed. I disclosed that the sales were good, but could be better. He told me while living in Denver he had several elite contracts with some Fortune 500 companies doing motivational speaking and he offered to run a morning meeting for my office, which I immediately accepted.

I prepped Pastor Lewis on a few of the people in the office I valued as major "players." These people not only were great in sales, but also had that special something that was needed to be able to effectively manage other people.

Marcus Henderson was a forty-two year old African-American man, who by all accounts had a mixture of street smarts and good looks. He was a professional hustler that now wanted to make money the "right way." Having worked in an Italian Restaurant for many years, Marcus was fluent in the language and had many connections within the Italian community. He had a polished appearance and was one of the most money-motivated people within the office. Marcus on any given week could profit over two thousand dollars in commission. But because of his hustling history, I was prone to spot-check his work for possible fraud. He always came out clean as a whistle.

If you looked in the dictionary under "people person," you would find Christopher Porter. He was a twenty-five year old Yugoslavian from New Jersey. He was strong in sales, consistently producing over a thousand dollars in commission a week, but desperately wanted to reach a management position. He consumed his day by training the new people. Christopher was clearly the most popular personality in the office and everybody loved him.

Self proclaimed "cleanup lady" was Sabrina York. She would challenge everyone in the office to make the most of their territories and if they didn't, she would go behind them a day later and still pull two or three hundred dollars going in the same doors that might have rejected them or by going into a door they skipped because of seller's intimidation. A single mother in her mid-thirties, she was an encouragement to many who thought a career in sales was too hard.

"Sounds like you have a lot of good people."

"I do, I must say, I do. But a good motivational meeting from you could make all the difference," I said, smiling. "Sometimes a different perspective is all that's needed."

"How often do you have meetings?"

"I manage a direct sales office so I feel it's necessary to run a motivational meeting on a daily basis." I paused, then added, "you know I need to warn you of something, my meetings are loud, active, and crazy. You will probably think you have entered a cult or

44

something, I know I did when I first witnessed one, but there is a method behind the madness." I said trying my best to warn him. "Tomorrow I will start the meeting by introducing the 'bell ringers,' those are people who made over three hundred dollars in sales the previous day. Each person will run around, slap hands, and end by telling the office what they did to have a financially successful day."

"That sounds pretty harmless," he chuckled.

"Yeah, it sounds harmless, but keep in mind I'm not talking, but screaming and the office chants and hoots. It's not a very dignified meeting, but they love it and it's a form of motivation." I said, laughing.

"Sounds like fun."

"It will be and after you see all of that, I'll introduce you."

"Good, I can't wait. How's your pasta?" He asked noticing I had only completed half of the dish compared to his empty plate that once held a large portion of lasagna and cheese garlic bread.

"It was good." I was slightly embarrassed that he had noticed I didn't eat much. I picked up a fork full of pasta and said, "I've just been enjoying talking to you." I was shocked that had come out of my mouth, but I had to cover up the actual reason of my lack of appetite - nervousness. He was wonderful in almost every way I could see, which only confirmed that he would be a great catch.

The evening was great. The food, the conversation, and more significant was the revealing of a human underneath the cloth. He actually ordered wine for us. I had no idea preachers consumed alcohol.

The check came and Pastor Lewis immediately grabbed it. He didn't even flinch when he saw the bill. My calculations put it at least seventy-five dollars. I had no idea that the restaurant was so expensive, but all in all it was worth it to me and judging from that constant smile

45

on his face, it was to him, too. He pulled out what appeared to be a Platinum Visa card and handed it to the waiter.

It was getting late and the conclusion of a great day was upon us. The subject of where he was staying had not come up. As we exited the restaurant he asked, "I wasn't able to get in contact with my old pal, Pastor Fuller in Queens. Would you mind if I crashed at your place since I'm conducting the meeting tomorrow morning?"

A sudden wave of heat ran through my body. I couldn't believe what he was asking. Yes, I had prepared for the possibility, but hearing him ask took me way off guard. I never really expected him to stay with me. Although it made sense for him to spend the night with me since he was running the sales meeting tomorrow morning, I still couldn't help having mixed emotions. It was evident there was some mutual attraction. The extent of his was still unknown, but it was there. Pastor Lewis had not come right out and professed his interest, but all the signs were there.

"Sure, by all means," I agreed.

The ride to my apartment was a quiet one. We talked on and off. We mainly listened to a jazz station I had preprogrammed, not knowing if he would find R&B acceptable. As I pulled into the parking lot of my newly constructed apartment complex, my heart began to race.

I unlocked the door and I was pleased to be greeted with the aroma of clean freshness. I had left a small antique lamp on that gave the room a cozy, yet romantic feel. I immediately walked into the kitchen to separate myself from the "what if's" and to gain my composure.

"Have a seat and make yourself comfortable. Would you like some juice or soda?" I asked as I poured a glass of Kool-Aid and consumed it in four swallows. My nerves were on edge, but I tried to remain cool and collected.

"No, thank you. I'm okay."

I walked into the living room finding him casually seated on the couch with his long legs crossed facing me as I walked in. I sat in the space he had left for me on the couch. He was less than six inches from me and I could still smell the sweet musk of his cologne. Looking directly at me he said, "You have a really nice place."

"Thank you, I'm just getting things organized the way I want. I still have some decorating to do."

We sat in silence for a moment and he made eye contact with me. He raised his hand and caressed my cheek. "You are so beautiful."

He slowly drew closer to me and kissed my lips, slowly at first, then parted his lips allowing his tongue to enter my mouth. This shocked me and I could feel my body tense. His hands supported my head as he drew himself closer to me. His lips were very tender and warm. He lowered his attention to the nape of my neck where he lightly kissed and then sucked. I was consumed with his touch and his smell. Becoming more relaxed, I moved my hands to his wavy hair and allowed my fingers to explore and revel in the feel of its soft texture.

In one motion he stood up while holding my hand and pulled me up to him. Pulling the small of my back into his waist, I could feel the hardness and thickness of his erection against my stomach. He explored my mouth with tremendous sensuality. I could feel his hands tightening around my head as he kissed me deeper, as if he couldn't get enough of me. He released me just enough to allow room for one of his hands to find the entrance to my blouse. He groaned as he discovered my now swollen nipple. I was hot all over.

He stopped kissing me and looked into my eyes, as if he was searching for something. It was a look I had never received before from any man. It was a look of extreme passion and desire. He raised his hands to the jacket of my suit and released it from my shoulders. His hand then went to my blouse, unbuttoning slowly until my lace bra was completely revealed. I allowed the shirt to fall to the floor. He unclasped the front of my bra allowing my now throbbing bosom to be exposed. He just stared at me. "You are so beautiful, you are so beautiful," he said in almost a whisper and started kissing me with vigor. Within a minute, our bodies were intertwined on the living room floor. His hands flowed from over my lips, to my neck, between my breasts and stopped at my stockings and panties. He pulled both down and began kissing my belly button. He moved downward to the essence of my femininity. I lay there shocked that he would do something so personal so soon. For minutes, he hungrily probed and licked between my legs as I moaned with desire. His tongue entered me and explored my walls and brought me to a point of immeasurable pleasure. He then worked his way up to my breasts, burying his head in each of them, caressing and sucking.

My body was aching for more. I needed him inside me or I would explode. His mouth found mine and we kissed while he positioned his manhood to enter me. With one thrust, he engulfed my being and it was a perfect fit. Moments later we lay in each other's arms. At that moment he was no reverend, no pastor, only a man that completed me.

The next morning, a muscular, hairy thigh rubbing my leg awakened me. I opened my eyes to confusion as I looked at the peaceful face of Pastor Lewis deep in slumber. For a moment I just lay there looking deeply at him. While sleeping, his features possessed an innocence that had no signs of the intense act that had taken place less than eight hours before. I gently raised my head to see the alarm clock positioned on the nightstand behind his head-5:18am.

My emotions were all over the place. How can I possibly look at him in the eyes, knowing what just happened. I just fornicated with my pastor. Lord, please forgive me. I closed my eyes to try and make some sense of what had gone wrong. I truly just messed up any future with him now.

I had taken a vow of celibacy and it had been six months. How did this happen?

But he was more than a pastor; he was a man that had feelings for me, which he demonstrated by passion that overwhelmed both of us. So, do I still call him Pastor Lewis? Do I call him by his first name, Kevin? I'd just follow his lead.

I had to go to the restroom and freshen up before he woke up. There's no telling what I looked like after last night. I slid out of bed and tiptoed into my restroom. I quietly brushed my teeth and washed my face. After washing off, I sprayed my beloved Victoria's Secret Juniper Mist on my stomach, chest and neck. I quietly walked back in the bedroom and covered my nakedness by slipping on an oversized t-shirt before slipping between the covers. It was strange that even though Pastor Lewis, I mean Kevin, had seen almost every nick and cranny of my body, I now felt uncomfortable with him seeing me naked.

I got myself in the cutest position I could imagine as I prepared to wake him. I turned over allowing my hand to lay across his back. Doing so, he slowly turned over and spooned me. This was going to be hard. It felt so good to be in his arms, like there was no other place I was meant to be. I prepared to make another attempt to wake him, then in a raspy voice he spoke, "How did you sleep last night?" as he kissed the back of my neck.

"I slept really good. What time is it?" I said as I released a fake yawn and rubbed my eyes playing the role like I just woke up.

"I don't know, must be early. The sun isn't up yet."

I raised my head and looked at the clock behind him, "I can't believe it's 5:35. We need to get up," I said looking at him.

"Okay, but not before I do this." He pulled me close to him and kissed me lightly, and then with more passion.

We showered together and dressed all in about twenty minutes. He wore the same suit he had worn yesterday, but to me it looked brand new. I wore a brown suit with a matching sweater and brown ankle boots. I had already chosen this ensemble, not knowing if I would see him for more than one day. We shared the bathroom mirror as I put on my earth-toned makeup and he trimmed his mustache. No one mentioned a word about the previous night, but it was evident that it occurred. Sexy smiles and stares were passed by both of us. It felt good, like I was a teenager again with my first love.

49

We made it to the office at 7:10am. Luckily, we were the first to arrive. I didn't like for any of my contractors to make it to the office before me. I felt that in order to set a good example, I should arrive first. It also gave me an opportunity to give Pastor Lewis a quick tour before they arrived. As we walked through the door, I turned on the lights and put on my Bee Gees Greatest Hits CD. I turned up the volume and said, "You might as well get used to it; we keep it loud around here."

"I get it, I understand, it's a form of motivation, gets the blood pumping, right?" He screamed, trying to be heard over the music.

I showed him the reception area and my office and we ended up in the meeting room.

"Now this is where our morning meetings are held. We've almost outgrown this space. I keep our office's weekly goals displayed on the dry erase board and I do a count down every day as part of the meeting."

"So, looks like you have a goal of 2000 units a week and you've accomplished a little more than half of that," he observed.

"Yeah, I normally set the goals a little higher than what I know we are capable of achieving. But for us to have so many people in the office, our production should be a little higher than it is now. Again, that's what you're here for," I smiled at him. We walked back towards the lobby of the office and met the first two people who had come in while we were in the meeting room. It was Christopher and Marcus holding a very loud, comical, and visually expressive conversation over the Bee Gee's *Jive Talking*.

I said to Pastor Lewis, "These are the guys I was telling you about. Get with both of them, individually. Do you remember what I told you about them?"

"I sure do." He said quickly as we were now right in front of them.

"Hey, guys I have a surprise for you today, this is Kevin Lewis. He flew in from Chicago and will be conducting the meeting." Pastor Lewis extended his hand and all three men immediately began to converse about hot spots in Chi-town. Apparently, both Christopher and Marcus had visited a few times.

This allowed me a few minutes to breathe. I went into my office, which looked somewhat foreign to me after an afternoon away. I had three messages, two from local papers who were probably interested in selling advertisements. One message from Janet stating the time she closed the office and that she scheduled fourteen interviews for today. She's awesome. I returned to the atmosphere of the lobby and judging from the sporadic yells of welcome, more people had come in. I noticed Pastor Lewis had Marcus cornered and engaged in a seemingly serious conversation. In the few minutes I had been away, they seemed to have connected. I figured they would. Hopefully, a power salesman was being transformed into a possible manager.

I started off my meeting a little reserved. It was hard to allow myself to fully let go and get into the role with my normal yells, screams and chants. Nevertheless, the office was unusually energized, which ignited something within me to be able to block out the glare of the handsome preacher I had made love with so passionately only hours before. Seeing him from the corner of my eye made me lose focus and gave me chills.

The office had done great in the field the day before, selling over 750 units. Naturally, I had worried about not being in the office to welcome the guys back from the field to detect and counteract any possible negatives, but they did great. Twenty people made over $200 each. My daddy always said that a true office operates like a well-oiled machine, with or without the boss being there. My office proved that at least for one day, it could.

"I would now like to introduce you to a friend of mine that I have had the pleasure of knowing for some time now. He is one of the nation's most demanded professionals. His talents have allowed him to speak at huge organizations like IBM, The Xerox Corporation, and AT&T. He is the author of *Your Best Self*. He pastors one of the fastest growing churches in the greater Chicago land area. And, ladies and gentleman, *we* got him." The office applauded and yelled. "I'm pleased to present to you, Mr. Kevin Lewis."

Sure, I exaggerated a bit, but this is a sales and promotions firm. Most of it was true. Pastor Lewis walked towards me and shook my extended hand. He warmed up by mentioning what a pleasure it was to meet the individuals he had met. He did so, calling each by name and mentioning something about each person he had found out through his morning conversations. After twenty minutes, he had spoken about being the best you can be, not settling for the mediocre or mundane and the importance of setting your sights high. He concluded with an exercise where he had everyone in the office to stand on a folding chair he had placed in the middle of the floor one by one. As each followed his direction, he shouted, "...now look around, you have a different perceptive about your surroundings just by raising above your normal present state. The air is better up there, you can see more up there, and you are above your competition up there." He shouted as he spoke directly to each person that stood on the chair. "I challenge each of you not to settle for the $1000 you can make a week. Yeah, that's good, but don't get lost in that. Look higher. Have you ever thought that if at least fifteen or twenty people in here are making that thousand dollars a week, what is Ms. Thomas making?" He asked as he pointed at me and smiled. Everyone's eyes widened.

Thunderous applause filled the room at the conclusion of his speech. He was practically mobbed by everyone in the office who just wanted to talk to him or shake his hand. I could hear Catrina Jackson and Portia Shields, two African-American ladies who were standing in line to shake Pastor Lewis's hand, conversing on how fine they thought he was. I just smiled.

"Natalie, you in there?" I was freshening up in the restroom, when I heard the knock. He called me Natalie and he sounded good doing it.

"Yes, I'll be out in a second." Everything was still in place and I was on cloud nine.

When I entered my office where Kevin was already seated, he got up and closed the door behind me and said, "Did I tell you how sexy you look today?"

The butterflies were back. I couldn't get enough of being around him and hearing him express feelings that I'd always hoped he had. As he looked at me with those sexy deep brown eyes, I blushed. "No, I don't think you mentioned it." Feeling a deep sense of gratification, I added, "I need to tell you thank you. Your meeting was powerful. Everyone including myself was spellbound and hanging on your every word. And the part about me and what my earnings were, that brought it all home."

"Yeah, that was great. They definitely seem to have a bigger picture. There should be some managers sprouted from that bunch soon. Just continue to nourish that hunger they have from time to time, Natalie. Sabrina, Chris, and Marcus are really good potential managers, truth be told you have an office full of really good, solid, professionals. You just need to remember, sales is a tough business and they need to be reminded of a bigger picture, at least for those that want it." He said as he sat on the arm of the chair directly in front of me. He was holding my hands and looking into my eyes. "You know you can count on me to do what I just did any time, just let me know."

"I will." I drew closer, unable to control what I had been yearning for all day. I had never been more attracted to him than I was at that moment. As we kissed it grew from slow and passionate, to desperate and hungry. He stood up and locked the office door. Returning to me, he gently lowered me onto my desk and laid his long torso on top of me. He kissed and sucked my neck until I pulled away. "A hickey at my age is not cute," I whispered into his ear. He laughed and nibbled my ear, slowly licking behind it then inserting his tongue. My whole body shivered and I let out a sigh of delight. I allowed him total access and control of my office and he took dictation.

Chapter Eight

He was excited when I invited him to sit in during my interviews. I introduced him as a regional manager and no one knew any better. It was fun and enlightening to get his input on each candidate. He definitely knew his stuff. We were on the same page on analyzing each potential candidate.

I informed Janet to lock the office and call me after the contractors returned from the field. I told her I would be working a full day tomorrow, besides a needed hour or two to take Kevin to the airport. She looked at me with a "have fun" look. Even though I never confided in her about my feelings for Pastor Lewis or our "involvement," she probably knew that he was more than just my "pastor." She was a very observant girl.

It was our last night together and I wanted it to be special, but I also wanted to find out more about him. I anticipated peeling the layers to find out who the real Pastor Kevin Lewis was. I had been attracted to the pastor, but from what I knew about Rev. Lewis thus far, I could easily fall in love with "the man."

I wanted to really show him a good time and give him a tour of newly discovered spots in the city he could enjoy, but I didn't know much since most of my time since arriving in New York was spent in the office. I took him to a mall near my office. While doing some window-shopping, he reached for my hand to hold. I couldn't remember the last time someone held my hand. It felt good. He then shared that he felt so free with me. Free to hold my hand in public and share his feelings without judgment. I didn't ask him to explain. It was just so good to hear.

We went to Puff Daddy's Restaurant, *Justin's*, for lunch. It was nice. I had taken three of my top selling distributors there as a bonus a couple of weeks ago. The atmosphere was upbeat and the food was good.

"Do you want children, Natalie?"

"Yes, I would love children. Hopefully, a boy and a girl." I said as I envisioned the man sitting across from me as being a strong candidate for making that a reality. "How about you? Would you like children?"

He picked up his glass of sweetened tea and took a long sip. There was about three seconds of silence. Then he said something that I could not have ever expected to hear, "I have a daughter."

He has a child. Now I need a sip of something, but this tea in front of me wasn't strong enough to tackle the brick that just hit me in the face. As long as I attended and worked in the church, I never heard nor saw a child.

"Oh, really, how old is she?" I asked, trying not to show how shocked I was.

"Skyler just turned two in December," he said, then finally made eye contact. There was a hint of embarrassment in his eyes.

"Does she attend Divine Baptist? I don't think I've ever seen her." I asked, trying hard to make the conversation seem more casual than the actual prying nature that lay underneath the questioning.

"No, she lives in Indiana with her mother."

I couldn't believe what I was hearing. There was still one question I had to ask. Was this Negro still married?

"Do you have a picture of her?" I felt a picture would disclose a lot. Is it a family photo? Will the woman have on a wedding ring?

"You know what..." He reached into his back pocket to retrieve his wallet and pulled out a picture, "this was taken about six months ago."

As I looked at the professional photo of the cute little girl, I observed that she had a light brown complexion. Her curly hair was pulled into a neat puff on top of her head with a blue ribbon to match the color of her sundress. She didn't resemble him at all, but was undeniably adorable.

"She's so cute, Kevin. Look at that little smile. She is just too cute. She must get her color from your ex-wife."

"Yeah, her mother's mixed with Black and Jewish."

Tired of wasting time I just asked, "How long were you married?"

"We weren't."

Okay, this was almost too much to consume over lunch. There's a young child. Not only a child, but a love child. There was a baby's momma. How can a pastor have all of this? It's not like this child was conceived before he was a saved man of God in the pulpit preaching the importance of living by the Ten Commandments, which prohibited fornication. She was two. She was conceived while he was the pastor of Divine Baptist Church.

Reading the confused look on my face he explained, "I met Shelby shortly after the passing of my dad. I was looking through the personals in Black Voices.com and saw her profile. It looked like we had a lot in common. She had earned her master's degree and was working as a professor of sociology at the University of Indiana. She was a few years older than me, but had never married. We started communicating through the chat rooms, then e-mails. After a while, I flew up to meet her and we started a relationship." He paused and reached across the table to caress my hand. "Looking back, I reached out to her in a vulnerable time in my life. Our involvement started out great, but over time it soured. We were looking for different things. She wanted a child and I didn't. On what was to be my last visit, we had a heated argument and she started to cry. She had been through so many bad relationships and she knew ours was ending, too. My heart went out to her and we made love, which conceived Skyler. When she told me she was pregnant, I was angry. I felt that she used me for what she ultimately wanted, a child. I supported her through the pregnancy and the birth. What surprised me most of all is when I first looked at

Skyler, I loved her with all the love in my soul and I couldn't and wouldn't deny her anything."

I examined his face. His eyes had filled with tears. My heart went out to this man, who simply got lost in the flesh. Having a child out of wedlock, while being a pastor, was apparently a secret he has kept close to him. I was surprisingly drawn to him for trusting me enough to disclose something so sacred.

Returning to the apartment that night, my feelings were just as strong, if not stronger. The truth about his past proved he was not perfect. He had come clean and exposed himself as a naked lamb in my presence. If he did not care, he could have easily kept Skyler and Shelby neatly locked in his closet.

At one time, I had viewed him as this unattainable creature of perfection, someone who was too holy and Godly to ever have any real interest in me. The truth of the matter was that I was still in my journey toward salvation. I was a good person, by most accounts, but I had flaws and had sinned. The fact that he had a child made me view him as someone that is not on a pedestal, but someone like me, imperfect.

I purposely chose not to bring up the past any more. I still wanted our last night to be special and a baby or baby's momma I haven't even met would not spoil our night.

We had a cozy night in front of the television watching *Pretty Woman*. I lay in his lap as he gently stroked my hair. By the end of the movie, I had fallen asleep. Waking up, I met eyes with Kevin who apparently was watching me sleep. Embarrassed, I sat up.

"Did you like the movie?" I asked.

"It was good, but I'd seen it before. I was just watching you sleep."

"Oh, my God, I hope I wasn't drooling." I asked, all of a sudden self-conscious.

"No, I don't think so." He rubbed his hand on his thigh, as if he were checking for a wet spot, "But you were sawing some major wood," he said as he laughed.

"No, I wasn't. Good try, but I happen to know I don't snore," I replied jokingly. It felt good to laugh with him.

"You wanna grab a shower before bed?" he asked.

"Sure," I responded without hesitation.

I went into the bathroom, turned on the water in the shower and lit a candle. I started taking off my clothes and Kevin entered the room already naked. The glimmer of the candlelight produced the perfect silhouette of Kevin's tall, muscle-toned body on the bathroom wall. I felt his hand on my shoulder, which triggered a shiver through my body. His hand then moved south to my bra strap, which he unclasped effortlessly. As the lace bra fell to the ground, I stepped out of its matching panties. We stepped into the shower and took turns lathering each other's body. His hard wet body looked so good in candlelight. I stood behind him and reached up to lather his neck, working my way down to his shoulders and back. I then lathered his buttocks and was turned on by their firmness. His long legs were equally sexy, displaying a slight bow I had never noticed before.

Surprised by my own boldness, I said, "Turn around," looking forward to doing his front. When he turned around we stood looking into each other's eyes. Neither of us saying a word, just looking, without lust, but with divine admiration and love. He brought his arms around my shoulders and slowly lowered his head to mine. He kissed me so gently, exploring my mouth with soft kisses. It was a while before I realized that he had been washing my back while kissing me. Pressing my body tighter into his, my body hungered for more of his touch.

After the shower, he dried me, then himself. I blew out the candle and he reached down to pick me up and carry me to my bedroom. After he laid me on my bed, he stood over me, as if he were examining me closely. I would normally feel self-conscious in a situation like this, but, amazingly I didn't. He sat down on the edge of the bed beside me and said, "Natalie, it's important for you to know I didn't come to New York to have sex with you. I have admired you from afar for months now, but just never said anything because with you being a member, it just wouldn't look good. That's why I was so glad to get your Christmas card. I didn't want to waste time to see you and to find out if you felt the same way. Do you?"

"Yes, Kevin I do. I really do," I said honestly.

As though he were relieved to hear my response, he let out a sigh and smiled.

"I'm so glad to hear that, Natalie." He hugged me and to my surprise whispered in my ear, "I care for you so much. I always have." That night we didn't have sex, yet we had already made love in so many ways.

Chapter Nine

I was behind on a lot of work. Although Janet had done all she was capable of doing, she had left stacks of papers consisting of resumes, applications, and sales summary sheets for the contractors, and messages from yesterday for me to review. I prioritized my stack and started with the resumes and job applications. The twenty people who came in yesterday were narrowed down to nine. The other eleven had limited sales experience, were too young or not polished enough.

"Janet, would you come in here a second, please?" Despite my workload I was in a great mood.

"Yes, boss. And how are you doing this morning?" She said, wearing a "I know what you've been doing" look.

"What's up with the Kool-aid smile?" I said, knowing exactly what she was smiling about. If the tables were turned, I would kid around about it, too.

"Oh, nothing. Could you understand the system I put your work in? I tried to keep all related items in the same pile."

"Oh, yes. Everything was great. Thank you for all of your help the past two days in my absence. I appreciate it."

"Not a problem — anytime. I would offer to do it more often, but if you glow anymore I'm gonna have to ask for a raise to afford some Ray-Bans up in here. Girlfriend, you look radiant," she said, shaking her head as if she were looking at a totally different person.

"You think so? Well, thank you. It was good to get away for a while," I said trying hard to downplay my happiness.

"Natalie, if you don't mind me asking, how do you know Mr. Lewis, again?"

"He's a friend of mine from Chicago," I said trying to look serious.

60

"And he's a pastor, too, right?" She added.

"Yes, Janet, he pastors a church in Chicago."

"He was the pastor of the church you attended while you lived there?" She pried.

"Yes, Janet."

"Okay…" she started walking to the doorway leading to the hallway and looked back and opened her mouth as if she was going to say something, but paused and said, "He's a handsome man, seems really nice, too, Natalie. If you were to date, I mean if there were interest there, you guys would make a stunning couple." She said wearing smile as she left the room.

It was a long day, but a good one. I conducted interviews and did a ton of paper work. After calculating the sales summary sheets, I realized two things. There was no one in the office that made less than six hundred and fifty dollars that week. Second, I needed a computer. It was time to upgrade. I was always frugal with company money, but with the office being as profitable as it was, there was no need for us to do all this paper work by hand.

"Natalie, sorry to interrupt you, but Mr. Lewis is on line for you." Janet buzzed in on the intercom.

"Thanks." My heart did that little flipping thing. I had been anticipating his call, but had refused to make the first move. I paused for a second to gain my composure. I wanted to come across cool and collected over the phone. I looked at the blinking light on the phone and I was nervous to pick it up.

"This is Natalie Thomas, how may I help you?"

"Hi, Natalie, it's Kevin." He sounded good.

"Well, hello there. You made it back okay?"

"Yeah, I just woke up from a nap and I'm about to go to the church and meet with the secretary before she leaves for the day. How are you doing?"

"Good, I've caught up on a lot. The office is still standing and life is good," I said meaning every word of it. "Hopefully, this will be the last Saturday I will have everyone work."

"How are Marcus, Chris, and Sabrina doing?"

"They are awesome. Everyone really enjoyed your meeting. If I remember correctly, they all made over a grand last week."

"That's awesome, Natalie! Listen I have to go. I just wanted to let you know that I really enjoyed myself. I'm making a reservation to come back next week around the same time. Is that okay?"

My heart skipped a beat. "Of course it's okay. I look forward to seeing you. Just let me know your flight info, so I can make arrangements to be away from the office." I was trying desperately to conceal my excitement. He's coming back!!!

"As soon as I know, I'll let you know. I'll call you tonight. Bye."

"Bye, bye." I hung up the phone, flying as high as a kite.

Chapter Ten

I stood with anticipation at LaGuardia Airport looking at the faces departing the plane as I had for the many other visits from Kevin. It seemed like once a week for the past few months, he would fly to see me for a few days. I couldn't help but feel special to know that such a busy man would take so much of his valuable time from the ministry to spend three days a week with me. Our relationship had grown from deep and passionate to a level of love I never thought I would experience.

He was dressed in faded, loose-fitting Levis and a long sleeved white shirt. No matter what he wore, he looked delectable. His eyes met mine and we both smiled. It's funny the butterflies I experienced in the beginning of our relationship had not faded, but instead it's like the butterfly wings had expanded. The more time I spent with him, the deeper my feelings had become.

He put his arms around me and squeezed me close to him. It was a type of hug that made me feel loved with the strength and length of it. He smelled good as always. He knew my favorite cologne was Isseymiyake. When he released me he gave me a brief, yet intimate kiss on the lips followed by a quick kiss on the cheek.

"Hey, Baby. I missed you." He said as he took my hand and headed towards the parking garage.

"I missed you, too. I picked up something for Skyler."

"You did?" he said, smiling at me with amazement.

"Yeah, I saw the cutest little outfit and I know she'll look adorable in it. It's in the car, you'll see."

"Sweetie, that was nice of you to do." He squeezed my hand.

I had made the decision to pick up something for Kevin's daughter to demonstrate my feelings for him and my acceptance of his child. It was a struggle for him to tell me about her mainly because of the fact that she was conceived out of wedlock, given the fact that he was a preacher. It was important for him to know that I accepted her despite the circumstances surrounding her conception and his position.

Once in the car, I pulled out the outfit in the plastic Nordstrom bag. As I revealed the denim outfit with matching hat, I could envision his cute little girl wearing it.

"Natalie, thank you so much. I really appreciate it. We'll have to call her tonight and tell her all about it. I don't know how much she'll understand, but she's pretty advanced for a two year old," he bragged. "As a matter of fact, I'm going to Indiana next week and I'll take it to her then. Thanks again, Natalie." He reached over and kissed me on the cheek.

Our conversation had finally gotten to the point where it flowed. Before we became comfortable with each other, I carefully thought out what I was going to say before I said it and he mentally weighed the pros and cons about communicating some of his feelings regarding topics we would discuss. The few months of our involvement had taken away all communication barriers to the point where we just flowed with it.

"You look happy," he said.

"I am, actually. My office is number three in sales and the vice president called me this morning."

"Natalie, that's great. Congratulations. You've been working hard. I'm so proud of you, Baby."

"Thank you, thank you, thank you," I said trying to concentrate on my driving. "He said that I am eligible for Rookie of the Year and manager's bracelet at the company's next R & R Executive Weekend."

"That's right. I remember your mentioning that to me — when is that again?"

"In about a month, on April twenty-fifth in the Bahamas. You can go, can't you?"

"Yes, I told you I wouldn't miss it for the world. With all this good news, we have to celebrate tonight," Kevin said seductively."

"I agree. What do you have in mind?" I asked.

"I'm sure we'll think of something," he said as he rubbed his finger gently up and down my arm.

Chapter Eleven

I had never been so nervous. Sitting there in the huge auditorium filled with a mixture of vice presidents, board of directors and managers from various offices across the country, I found comfort by looking to the handsome man to my left who was slowly stroking my arm, sensing my nervousness.

"It is now time for the bracelet presentation. The bracelet is awarded to the manager who produces the most sales in their rookie year." Lawrence Silverberg was the CEO and spoke in a relaxed tone.

I had reviewed my numbers several times and compared them to all of the other rookies and was 98% sure I had earned my bracelet. I was confident that my name would be called. The fact that my promoting manager had called me to make sure I had purchased my ticket to come to the Bahamas was a sure sign the word had gotten out I was the "chosen one."

"The recipient of this years bracelet and the Rookie of the Year bragging rights is a young lady who has impressed us to no end." Kevin squeezed my hand. "Her office in New York has over fifty distributors and their quality of representation of our valuable clients has given them the opportunity to test market many prospective clients without worry. Through it all, this office generates no less than one hundred thousand dollars in any given week." The room burst in gasps and applause. "It is my pleasure to present this years bracelet and Rookie of the Year honors to Natalie Thomas."

I felt a rush of heat hit my face. I turned my head to meet the proud eyes of Kevin who kissed me on my cheek and whispered, "Congratulations, Baby."

I carefully stood and made my way down the aisle to the stage where Mr. Silverberg congratulated me with a small embrace and a kiss on the cheek. He handed me an open jewelry box displaying an elegant gold bracelet.

I approached the podium, gained my composure and shouted, "I would like to dedicate this acknowledgment to the best office in America," raising the jewelry to the air. "I am blessed to work with some great, hard-working individuals who make me look good. It is those people I would like to share this with. Thank you for the recognition and this beautiful bracelet."

The audience applauded and I saw a few familiar faces on their feet giving me a standing ovation. My original manager, Harry Bell, was applauding proudly while looking around smiling to his manager colleagues, as if he were a proud papa at his daughter's college graduation. He was obviously taking credit for his contribution to the companies newest star and bottom line. Kevin was on his feet sporting a sexy smile giving me the thumbs up between his vigorous applause. As I made my way from the stage and into the audience, I shook extended hands of congratulations and felt pats of well wishes on my back. Reaching my seat, I walked into the arms of Kevin's embrace and when he finally let go I noticed the wetness of his eyes looking down into mine. "I'm so proud of you, Natalie." He kissed me gently on my welcoming lips. That was the icing on the cake that sealed one of the best days of my life.

That evening we attended the company's Fireworks Extravaganza. I wore a pink and black bikini with a sheer pink wrap around my hips. Kevin's expression when I stepped out the bathroom proved to me what I already knew about my wardrobe selection. It was hot. He was seated on the couch wearing a white polo and blue shorts. He stood up, walked towards me and kissed me on the cheek.

"You look gorgeous."

"You don't look too bad yourself, Pastor," I said as I gave him a gentle peck on the lips. "It's not too much is it?" I was referring to my bikini top. It wasn't skimpy by any means, but being a 36C presented a challenge at times and I still wanted to be presentable.

He took a small step back and looked at me from head to toe, then smiled. "No, you look wonderful."

"Good, but before we leave for the beach, I want to call my parents to tell them about my day. They are going to be so excited for me."

"Sure, go right ahead," Kevin said as he returned to the bed to read the Wall Street Journal he picked up earlier. Even that turned me on. A man that read the paper has always been sexy to me.

"Hello?"

"Hi, Momma. What ya doing?"

"Just finished cooking some fish and fried green tomatoes. How's your trip?"

"Grreeeaat, I won the Rookie of the Year Award and was given the Bracelet of Achievement."

"You did whattt!!! Edward." She screamed. "Pick up the phone, Natalie won Rookie of the Year. Nat, that's great. Look at my baby. I'm so proud of you," my mother screamed.

"What is this I hear about my daughter winning Rookie of the Year?" My dad interrupted my mom by picking up the other line.

"Yep, I won. I wasn't sure I would win, but I did!"

They were both talking at the same time. I couldn't help but to get misty. Nothing on this earth made me happier than making my parents proud of me. I was so into their excitement, I hadn't noticed Kevin had walked behind me and wrapped his arm around my waist showing his endearment.

I quickly filled them in on all the meetings, events, and especially the beauty of the island. My parents had not traveled much at all, so I was their eyes to all the places I would go.

"I sent y'all some post cards yesterday, so you can see it for yourself, it's amazing. I have to go because there's a fireworks event on the beach that I'm running late for, but I had to call you to let you know about my day. I'm flying out tomorrow, so I'll call you when I make it back to New York."

The night was magical. After a vast buffet dinner consisting of rib-eye steak, prime rib, sautéed jumbo shrimp, salmon, and three types of salads, Kevin and I walked hand in hand along the sandy beach, which displayed the most beautiful tropical backdrop.

"It really warmed my heart to witness your enthusiasm talking to your parents," he said as he pulled my hand gently to stop our leisurely walk.

"It was great telling them. They were so happy. There's nothing better than that." I was smiling ear to ear remembering the excitement in both their voices.

"I would love to meet them," he said in a quiet voice, looking downward.

It warmed my heart to hear him say that. The man I loved wanted to meet my parents. Could it get any better?

"I would love for you to meet them. They would love you."

He was quiet for a second and just looked and asked, "Who do you look like, your mom or dad?"

"People have said both. My color is a mixture of theirs. People have said I have a figure like my mom, but I'm a little taller. A smile and dimples like my dad." I paused, pointing quickly at my cheeks and then looked downward shyly and added, "You'll have to judge." He had an unusual way of making me feel extremely confident one minute and like a little shy, awkward ten-year old child the next.

I looked forward to the day Kevin would meet my parents. My mom would fall in love with his intelligence and good looks. My dad would get a kick out of the fact that he was a preacher and that Kevin was easy to talk to and joke around with.

After a couple of hours of mingling with all the vice presidents, mangers and guests, we headed to our room to spend our last night full of passionate love making and romance on the island of the Bahamas.

Chapter Twelve

It was great being back in the office again. While I was in the Bahamas, I had Janet run the meeting and get the guys organized for the day. She had become such a great help to me, stepping in when I was away on trips with Kevin or attending speaking engagements at other offices. The team really liked her ability to be one of the guys, yet put them in place all in the same breath.

The team was highly charged with thunderous applause when I stepped in the meeting room holding my Rookie of the Year plaque. It was important for me to let them know that the acknowledgment was just as much theirs as it was mine. Scanning the crowd, we were missing about three familiar faces, but they were replaced with about five new ones.

The topic of my meeting was "Taking Your Sand To the Beach." I scanned the room and made eye contact with everyone in the room. "Less than a year ago, I was standing in a room similar to this one in Chicago. I was new to the direct sales business, new to the crazy highways, and new to working on commission. The one thing that wasn't new was my desire to achieve, my desire for success and my desire to make money. I was willing to put all of what was foreign to me aside and do whatever it took for me to accomplish what I knew was up to me and no one else to do — finish the training program. So for six months, I dedicated my life to achieving something I felt was greater than I had at that time and it worked."

All forty sets of eyes were hanging on my every word, tears filled mine. "It was a sacrifice, but I made it and you can too. Why, because I am braver, smarter, talented, or educated than you? No, the only thing that separates us is my hunger and commitment. If you feel you are as hungry and committed as me, great. There's nothing I would love more than to see you in the Bahamas with me next year. The simple fact is some of you will let the nature of the sales business, the negatives, or commission be your reason for quitting. For those that don't, I brought back a souvenir for each of you."

Perfectly timed, Janet walked in with a huge bucket full of small individually wrapped bags of sand I collected on my trip, secured with red ribbons. "For those that don't give up, I'll meet you in the Bahamas next year. You will be a manager and I can see you release this bag of beach sand on the shore under the tropical skies." The office roared with yells, hoots and hollers as each one ran up to grab their bag of sand, motivated to build on their tomorrow — today.

"Girl, you were great in there." Janet said as she came in with a cup of coffee for each of us.

"Thanks, it's great to be back. It's strange, but I really missed the office and all the guys."

"How did you find the time between your meetings and spending time with yo man to do the sand thing? That was nice." Janet and I had become really good friends, so we had both let our guards down enough to be "real" with one another. She still respected me as her boss and I still valued her as a wonderful employee.

"I thought about the idea while Kevin and I were walking along the beach. He helped me fill each individual bag before he flew back to Chicago."

"Things seem to be getting serious between you two."

"I have to admit, yeah, it's getting critical."

Janet laughed, "Honey, Ray Charles can see that, as much as he calls you everyday and as many trips he makes up here."

"Now you said he has a child, right?" She asked as she lifted the steaming cup of Folgers to her lips.

"Yes, she's two."

"Have you met her?"

"Not yet, but he says he's planning a visit for us to meet," I said, trying to sound confident.

"When?"

"Soon. I know he already has a trip planned up there this weekend, so it will be soon after that," I said, feeling disappointed by the unsure tone of my own voice.

"Oh, okay. Has he ever mentioned why his marriage failed?" She probed deeper.

"He has never been married." I said making every attempt to sound unphased by the comment I just made. I knew this was opening up a can of worms.

"Hold up, wait. Your boyfriend, who happens to be a preacher, has a child out of wedlock?" she said, looking shocked, but also smiling in disbelief.

"Look, I know what you are thinking. I thought the same when he first told me, but it ain't like that." I paused, trying to find the words. "Yes, he's a preacher, but he's also a man and he was tempted. Truth be told, I think the lady trapped him."

"I didn't know all of that," she paused, "but you seem to be okay with it."

"I am. Of course, I would love to have the ideal situation where I was dealing with a man without a child, but he does have one. In all honesty, Janet, what man at our age does not have at last one or two babies somewhere?" I asked looking her in the eye, proud of the point I just made.

"You definitely have a point, but he's not any guy, he is a preacher. How does his congregation feel about this?"

"He said they know and no one has made any waves about it."

"You believe him?"

"Yes, I do believe him."

Janet sighed and stood to her feet. "Just be careful." She walked to the door and turned around to ask, "You attended his church when you lived in Chicago, didn't you?"

"Yeah," I responded, suddenly feeling uncomfortable about the whole conversation.

"Did you ever see or hear about this child when you were there?"

"No," I said, breaking eye contact, bringing my attention to the papers on my desk. "I didn't, but I wasn't in the loop, so I wouldn't have heard, but I never saw her, either."

With that Janet gave me a comforting smile and was gone, leaving me alone in my office to catch up on paperwork and the unpleasantness of possible deception and delusion.

Chapter Thirteen

The week flew. I felt energized by the previous R&R Weekend and the office reflected it. Sales were steady and I hired four new people. I was looking forward to the weekend. This would be the first full week in a month that Kevin would not fly down for his weekly Thursday through Saturday visit. I anticipated lounging in my Victorias Secret pajamas, cleaning my apartment and watching a few rented movies.

On my way home from the office, I stopped by the RANDALL'S and picked up a fillet of salmon and a bottle of Arbor Mist wine. Blockbuster Video didn't have any new releases I wanted to see, so I picked up *Love Jones* and *Shawshank Redemption*. I had seen them both, but they were still worthy of the seven dollars to see again.

While the fish was sautéing, I gave Kevin a call on his cell phone. I figured he should have made it to Indianapolis by now to visit Skyler. After four rings, his voice mail message came on. "This is Pastor Kevin Lewis, I am not available, but please leave a message. I will return your call at my earliest convenience. May God bless you. Beep."

"Kevin, this is Natalie. Call me when you get this message."

He should definitely be there by now. He's normally really good about calling me, except when he goes on his visits. I always seem to have to call him, only to get his voice mail. I have to keep reminding myself not to be so demanding for his routine calls when he's with his daughter. He doesn't see her very often, so I have to learn to adapt to a man who is responsible enough to spend quality time with his child.

The salmon was all but a memory and Morgan Freeman had reunited with Tim Robbins by the time I received my call.

"Hello?"

"Hey, Natalie. How are you?" He asked in a sleepy voice.

"Good," I replied, trying not to sound upset that he was just now calling me. "Were you asleep?" I asked.

"Yeah, I crashed. Skyler wore me out. She's at that age, you know?" he said as he yawned.

"I've always heard about the terrible twos. I'm sure she's just happy to see her daddy," I said smiling, trying to imagine Kevin playing with his daughter.

There was a few seconds of silence and I said, "Listen, it's late, you sound beat, so get some rest. Hold on a second, so I can grab a pen to get the number to the hotel."

"I'm staying at Shelby's."

Hearing that was like a getting run over by a eighteen-wheeler truck. What the hell is going on? My mind started to wonder about all the negative possibilities. I always heard about the connection two people have when they share a child. Is that why he was speaking so quietly, not to have Shelby hear any of his conversation?

"At Shelby's? Why?"

"I'm sleeping on the couch, Natalie. I don't have anything to hide from you. There's absolutely nothing and hasn't been anything between Shelby and me for some time now. She's the mother of my child and that's it," he said in a definitive tone as though to end further discussion.

That wasn't going to work. He wasn't going to use his manipulation to control my thoughts of the situation or response to it.

"I don't have to tell you that I'm very uncomfortable with that, do I?" I said, trying to remain calm.

"Look, Nat. I had no idea you would feel this way. It's already close to eleven. Can we just discuss this tomorrow? I'll be flying back to Chicago in the morning."

"Fine, not a problem," I said dryly.

"Talk to ya later, bye."

"Bye."

No "I love you" this time, and I wasn't about to tell him I loved him first to draw one out. That was the driest conversation we had ever had. I often heard of the eternal connection between the parents of a child and how each would always carry with them the memory of sexual experiences, passion and the bond of that child which symbolized it all.

As I lay in bed, I tossed and turned, thinking of Kevin holding, caressing, kissing, or making love to the mother of his child. Although I trusted him, I knew that this was a possibility and there was nothing I could do about it. Does he always sleep at Shelby's when he visits? It's a question I never thought to ask. It's one that never came up because I always assumed he was staying at a hotel the couple of other visits he made. It was only now that I asked and now was sorry I did.

I didn't wake up until close to ten on Saturday morning, which was strange because I could usually never sleep past eight. Kevin was still heavily on my mind, but I tried to keep myself busy by washing clothes and mopping my kitchen. It was after two o' clock when my phone rang. I looked at my caller id to see that it displayed Divine Baptist Church.

"Hello," I said trying to sound as busy as possible.

"Hey, what are you doing?" Kevin asked sounding more chipper and alert than the previous night.

"Just doing some cleaning. You made it back to Chicago?"

"Yeah, I landed about an hour ago. I just made it to the church in enough time to prepare for the new member orientation I have in about fifteen minutes."

"Okay." I was deliberately going to be short with him.

"About last night, I'm sorry for not talking to you longer, but I called after Skyler fell asleep on my chest and I didn't want to wake her."

"Not a problem, but why didn't you tell me you were planning to spend the night at Shelby's?"

"I just assumed you already knew. Every time I fly into Indianapolis, it's for such a short period of time and I try to get as much time as possible with Skyler out of each trip, so I sleep on Shelby's couch."

"So the other times you visited, you stayed there, too?"

"Yes. I told you that I don't see Skyler much and Shelby refuses to put her on a plane to fly her to Chicago, so I need to get as much time with her as I possibly can. I barely see my child and that's hard enough. It's very difficult to deal with Shelby when it comes to our child. It's like it's her way or the highway."

"So, let me get this right. Shelby dictates what she wants and you go along with it?" I was getting angry.

"Unfortunately, yes. That's how's it been since Skyler was born and I don't like it."

"Have you ever thought that she's using Skyler as a way to keep you close to her? Does she still have feelings for you, Kevin?" I had asked the questions so abruptly without thinking how they might come out.

"You know," he paused, "I can't and I won't get into this with you now. Apparently, you are too consumed about how this affects you without being sympathetic about what hell I'm faced with just trying to have a relationship with my own daughter." He said angrily. "I need to let you go, so I can pray before these people come in here. I'll call you later."

He hung up the phone. I had pissed him off. I was trying to understand, but I had questions and concerns of my own. He should understand that. Women have always tried to trap men into involvements by using a child and how do I know this lady is any different? I don't.

I had cabin fever. I was tired of the routine of going to the office and coming home. All of my free time was spent with Kevin or thinking about him. I looked at the clock and saw the time of 7:15pm. Reaching for my cell phone, I scrolled down to see find Janet's home number.

"Hello?"

"Janet, it's Natalie. What are you doing tonight? I'm bored."

"Not much. You wanna grab a bite to eat, or something? I heard of this new soul food resturant about five blocks from the office, on Henderson. You wanna meet up there?"

"Sounds like a plan. In about an hour?" I got directions, grabbed a quick shower and was out the door in thirty minutes.

* * *

"I would like the smothered pork chops, please." I gave the obese young lady my order.

"You get two sides with that," she said in a monotone voice, as if she were ready to get off work.

"Okay, I'll take the collard greens and black-eyed peas." The place was crowded and everyone who had their plates had one goal on their mind — devouring their food. The only people talking were those who didn't have their orders.

"Okay, let me make sure I've got it. One chitlin dinner and one smothered pork chop, would that be all?" she said as she smacked her gum.

"Yes, thank you."

"So, what's been up with you, boss?" Janet was wearing a fashionable black blouse that revealed one shoulder with black jeans. She was also carrying a new coach leather purse. She was always well put together, with the newest styles and fashions.

"Same old stuff. I just had to get out and be around people other than the guys at the office and Kevin," I said as I took a sip of the sweetened tea the waitress had just put in front of me.

"Amen to that." She looked to notice two men who came in and smiled towards our table. "How are you and Mr. Lewis doing?" she asked, directing her attention back to me.

"Good, well, it's just hard, with the distance thing, you know?"

"Yeah, I did the distance thing before and it was hard." She reached to grab a hush puppy from the wicker basket the waitress put in the center of our table, "I tell you one thing, you can still pull them. Those guys that just walked in can't stop looking over here at you."

I sneaked a quick peek and said, "Those men are not looking at me, they're looking at you."

"Why don't you ever give yourself any credit? You are an attractive woman, why do you find it so shocking that a handsome brother could be checking you out?" she asked.

"Can we change the subject?"

It was difficult to come to grips with, but she was right. I still carried insecurities from my youth about my looks. Granted, I looked better now than ever before, but that little girl that was always too skinny or too dark was always there.

The next couple of hours were spent with me laughing more than I'd laughed in months. We talked about everything from politics to what we were looking for in men. We both realized we had one thing in common in visiting our ghosts of past loves. We were both very giving people who were filled with a lot of love, but could not seem to find a man that was looking for the same. Our past four to five years were spent going from relationship to relationship, each one ending in disappointments. Janet could not help but laugh when I told her about Darren.

Darren was thirty years old, 6'4", and had a great job. He told me he had never been married and didn't have any children. In the beginning of our involvement, Darren was all about me, calling me, sending me roses, opening my doors, taking me to concerts. Anything I wanted to do, we did. Anywhere I wanted to go, we went. He was the perfect guy with great credit. Darren was so fine, that anywhere we went, the ladies would check him out, but his eyes stayed on me. Perfect man, huh? Not. As it turned out, Darren was the perfect con man/actor. Darren was a convicted criminal, fresh out of jail. The good job I thought he had turned out was delivering pizza for Dominoes. All the dates to concerts and dinner were paid for on a credit card that was stolen from Darren's ex-wife. She apparently filed charges when she was trying to buy groceries for her and their six children and she realized the credit card was gone. That's when she hired a private investigator who paid me a visit, shortly thereafter.

"Girl, no. That didn't happen." She was laughing hysterically.

"Yep. It did. The sad thing is that ain't the only loser, either. There's been more, but it'll take all night. I'm beginning to think there's a tattoo on my forehead that reads, "If you are a man that is unavailable emotionally, a player, ex-con, or not looking for anything serious, please step to me.""

Janet was laughing so hard, she nearly spilled her tea. She reached across the table and gave me a high five. "Girl, ain't that the truth. I'm beginning to think I'm sending off the wrong type of vibe."

"Maybe we are. All I know was I got down on my knees and prayed for the Lord to send me my Adam. I want to be married. I want to be loved and I want to love someone. That's all. I don't think that's too much to ask for, do you?"

81

"Not at all. Do you think the Lord sent you Mr. Lewis?"

"I hope so. I really hope so. He has some good traits and a few that I have to pray about. But, no one is perfect. I know I'm not. If he was sent by God, I want to make it work."

Chapter Fourteen

I picked up Harry Bell from JFK Airport early Friday morning. He flew in to give support and join in the celebration of the promotion of my first Assistant Manager in my office. Christopher Porter would be promoted today. Affectionately called "The Yugoslavian Mule" around the office, he had been the first to reach a management position by personally training ten individuals who were all producing over a $1,000 a week. Out of those ten, five were definite leaders in the office and in a position of training others, as well.

This day was sure to be an emotional one for Christopher because his unstoppable work ethic had fueled his situation to reach the level he had dreamed of since he started with me a little over six months ago. He had that magnetic positive attitude that made him clearly the office favorite. Everyone loved Christopher and because of his positivity, determination and the profitability his presence and energy brought to the office, I did too.

This would be my first promotion, so I had planned everything to the letter. I dropped Kevin off at the office before my drive to pick up Harry. Kevin had flown in the night before and insisted on not missing the promotion because he had been very impressed with Christopher and knew it was a huge accomplishment for me to have trained someone who would now be recognized company-wide as an Assistant Manager.

Kevin's job was to arrange all the refreshments, put up the decorations and organize the troops as they came in. Christopher, even though he knew he was getting close to management, had no idea he and his team had reached his production goal, solidifying his promotion. I told him to be at Kinko's at 8:30 to pick up some documents I had dropped off the day before, placing him at our office at 8:45.

Harry Bell was addressing the office, when Janet stuck her head in the meeting room signaling Christopher's red Ford Mustang had just pulled in the parking lot.

"Excuse me, Harry," I whispered into my mentor's ear and I then turned to the fifty-something highly anticipated faces, speaking louder. "The man of the hour has just pulled into the parking lot. Remember, everyone remain calm until after the meeting officially promoting Christopher." Everyone tried to conceal their smiles.

A few seconds later, the door eased open. Christopher walked in, noticed the decorations and lowered his head in what seemed to be a combination of shock and embarrassment, realizing it was all for him.

"Christopher, take your place right over there," I pointed to a space next to Kevin.

He slowly walked over and took his place, shaking Kevin's hand, noticing he had made the trip to celebrate the day.

I took a breath and made eye contact with Kevin, as if to muster strength for words. This was as momentous for me as it was for Christopher and I needed to find just the right words to articulate the significance of the moment and, most importantly, his accomplishment.

"Christopher, it's been a little over six months since you joined us. Within that time you have demonstrated a strong work ethic consisting of perfect attendance, top sales performance, and the training of others. You've faced each day with a positive attitude and in turn you've gotten positive results. You have unselfishly trained several people in this room, making them your priority, and in doing so, resulting in a strong, profitable and positive team who adore you." I took a second to scan the room.

"Christopher, there are a few people standing to my right who made special arrangements to be here today. The gentleman who gave me my start, Harry Bell, flew in from Chicago. Next to him we have two other managers from the states of New Jersey and Massachusetts, Fred Jones and Doug Newsome," I said as I stood back while introducing each.

"Last week you and your team reached your production goal, officially earning you the title Assistant Manager. It is my pleasure to present you this plaque as a symbol of your new level with the company. Everyone, your new Assistant Manager, Christopher Porter."

The office exploded with thunderous applause and Christopher tried to reach me to accept his plaque, but was intercepted by everyone in the office with embraces. After a couple of minutes a newly promoted, teary-eyed Assistant Manager made his way to the front of the room and hugged me so tight, I felt every emotion he was feeling. He took his plaque, gave a quick, yet heartfelt thanks to his team and me, then shook the hands of Harry Bell and the two other managers.

I repeated what Harry had done with me on the day I was promoted and invited Christopher to spend the day in the office. For lunch, I treated Christopher, Harry, Fred, Doug and Kevin to *Bistro's*, one of Manhattan's most popular Italian restaurants. It was a lunch filled with management stories, goals, and current events. Everyone was aligned with similar viewpoints. Christopher was definitely the life of the party. His hyper energy was contagious across the table and everyone was at ease and equally talkative. Even Kevin, although not in the business, had enough general knowledge to make some positive contributions. He sat next to me, rubbing his foot against my leg. I was telling the other managers the story of my early days in the business and I could feel Kevin's eyes on me. I got warm all over. I then felt a hand on my thigh inching upward towards my femininity. I started to throb. I knew with the high I was on and the attentiveness of Kevin, tonight would be a magical night of passion.

It was almost eight o'clock when Kevin and I entered my apartment. As I walked into the bedroom to undress, he made a detour in the restroom, where I heard the shower start. He returned and finished undressing me, pulling off my slacks, pantyhose and underwear all with one motion. With my eyes closed, I stood there extremely turned on and totally at his disposal for him to have his way with me. His hand shocked me as I felt it move between my legs to massage my wet island and then enter it. He removed his moist hand and licked his fingers. Whispering in my ear, he gasped and said, "You taste so good."

He led me to the shower, where we talked about the excitement of the day. Between passionate kisses, we lathered each other's bodies. I always got so turned on to see his tall, brown body wet and bare. I was the luckiest woman in the world. To have a man so handsome, intelligent, spiritual, and so "into" me was more than I could ever dream.

After the shower, we slowly dried each other off. He led me to the bed where he laid me down. Still standing over me he caressed me with his eyes from head to toe. Strangely, I felt insecure with him looking at me so closely. I reached for his hand and pulled him on top of me. He leaned up on his elbow and looked in my eyes. There were tears in his. "I'm in love with you, Natalie. I am in love with you."

"I love you too, Kevin. I love you so much."

We kissed and worshipped every orifice of each other's body with sweet love. He caressed my belly, my thighs, my toes, my fingers, my navel, my knees, even my elbows with his hands, fingers, tongue, and lips all night long. This would be the man I would marry and I was convinced he felt the same.

Chapter Fifteen

"How are the guys' sales looking for this week, Janet?" I asked. The guys were still consistent in their sales after Christopher's promotion two weeks ago, but I wanted to make sure everything was okay.

"Looking good. Looks like the lowest income for this week is $540. That was made by..." she paused to look through her paperwork, "Jill Jackson, but she's the new girl that just started, isn't she?"

"Yeah. So, all is well. If a brand new, twenty-one year old, with very limited outside sales experience can make over $500 in her first week — that's good."

I was happy everything was still okay. Since Christopher's promotion, I had trained him on interviews, paperwork, conducting meetings, phones and office goals. I let him test the waters solo to get the hang of everything when I went away for a few days.

I had spent a few days last week in Tulsa with Kevin. He invited me out there to meet his three sisters. They were very nice and each successful in her own right. One was an accountant and the other two were engineers. They all had families and all could have been old enough to be my mother, but we connected and Kevin confirmed they really liked me. It felt nice to see Kevin open his world to me to meet his family. I still longed to meet his daughter, which I communicated to Kevin all the time. He would just say he's trying to work a meeting out with the mother.

I decided to send Christopher in the field to train a few reps on a new promotion our office was chosen to test market. He was eager to do so. He realized every new account would add an additional $30 to his $800 a week I was paying him as a salary, now that he was an assistant manager on payroll.

"What do you want me to order for lunch, Natalie?" Janet asked.

"It doesn't really matter. Is Chinese okay with you?" I wasn't really hungry, but it was approaching lunchtime.

"Anything's okay with me. You want your regular order of garlic chicken?"

"Yes, that's fine. Just let me know what time it will be ready and I'll go pick it up as soon as I finish this report," I said as I picked up the phone to call Kevin.

I called the church and his secretary greeted, "Divine Baptist Church. How may I direct your call?"

"Hello, Sister Douglas. Is the pastor there?"

"Well, hello, Natalie. He is here, hold on and I'll connect you:" Sister Douglas had been hired after I left, so I had never met her and she had no idea I attended the church, unless Kevin had told her.

"Divine Baptist Church, Pastor Lewis speaking, how may I help you?" His voice was strictly business.

"Hey, it's me."

"Hey, hold on for a second." I could hear him put the phone on his desk and say, "...look, you have to be more on your game. Brother and Sister Kennedy pay their tithes religiously, like clockwork. I cannot have you ruffling their feathers over some nonsense. He is a lawyer with a lot of connections and she's an assistant principal at one of the largest high schools in Chicago. They are doing more for outreach than most people are, bringing people in here on a weekly basis. If you piss them off, not only do their monthly tithes of over $1,200 go out the door, but their connections to other possible members and tithers leave, too. You have to think, my brother. I'm not going to have your ego stagnate the bottom line of my ministry. You understand?" I didn't hear a response, but I heard a door close a second later.

"You still there?" He sounded stressed when he returned to the phone.

"Yes, what was that all about?"

"These crazy elders of the church feel they can act like they are better than everyone. Not in my church." He was obviously angry. "We are all one under the covenant of God. They forget that a church is a business and we've got bills to pay and they have to learn to think about that at all times, especially when we are growing. Every tither counts," he vented.

"Who were you talking to? Is he okay?"

"Yeah, he's okay. That was Deacon Bailey. He'll be all right. You doing okay?"

"I'm fine. I'm working on this report and about to get me and Janet our lunch," I said as I was still trying to make sense out of what I just heard.

"I have to cut it short, because I have a meeting downtown. I'll call you later. Love you."

"I love you, too."

Thirty minutes later, I walked in with a garlic chicken for me and a sweet and sour chicken for Janet. After I gave her the entree, I headed into my office to finish the report. The Chinese was good, but I wasn't really hungry, so I picked over it as I looked up the information for my report. I tried to eat as much as I could, since I had paid five bucks for it, but I suddenly felt stuffed and sick to my stomach. I pushed the styrofoam container away, but the strong garlic smell that I usually loved made my nauseous. I tried to concentrate, but I felt like I was going to vomit. I took a sip from my Sprite to settle my stomach, but that triggered a gag reflex and I began to cough uncontrollably. My eyes filled with water to the point my vision was blurred and I struggled to feel for the trashcan closest to my desk. As soon as I grabbed it, my lunch poured from my mouth into the can. Not all at once, but in increments divided by coughs and gasping for air. I heard Janet yell from her desk, asking if I was okay, but I didn't have the air to respond. Seconds later, she ran in to find me on all fours hugging the trashcan, coughing, heaving, releasing all of what was inside me.

"Oh, my God, Natalie," Janet said as she bent down beside me and rubbed my back as if to comfort me through this now public scene. A few seconds later, I was able to get my balance enough to stand and sit back at my desk. Exhausted, I laid my head on my desk, wondering what had triggered that.

"Janet, I'm okay. Thanks for coming in to see about me, but I'm fine now." I hoped she got the point I wanted to be alone. I was already embarrassed and didn't necessarily want her looking up side my head wondering what was wrong with me.

"No, no you aren't. You look horrible, let me go wet a paper towel for your eyes."

I pulled my head up enough to look in my desk drawer for a mirror. My shaking hand pulled out my small compact, which reflection revealed red eyes and a perspiring face. What just happened? I've always heard of people getting a hold of "bad" Chinese, but I had eaten at this restaurant for months and never had a reaction like this.

Janet reappeared with the damp paper towels, handed them to me and sat across the desk facing me. "Are you okay?"

"Yeah, now I am." Wiping my face with the cool towels and then pressing them to my eyes. "How was your food?"

"Okay. The same as always," she said, looking at me with concern.

"I don't know what triggered that. I'm just glad it's over," I said reaching for the Sprite to moisten my now dry mouth.

Janet leaned over the desk and supported her face with her hands and asked, "You don't think you're pregnant, do you?" Janet was always a straight shooter, never holding back questions or thoughts. It was a question I didn't want to hear, knowing it was a possibility, given the fact that I wasn't on birth control and Kevin often "pulled out" instead of using a condom. "I don't know. I sure hope not." I said softly.

"Have you missed your period?"

It's sad to say, I had no real idea. My schedule was always so busy; I didn't keep track of it. I then remembered making a comment to Janet last month, when she asked if I had a tampon, realizing our cycles were now at the same time.

"When was your cycle, Janet?" I asked.

"Last week."

All of a sudden I felt feverish all over. "I'm late. I just realized I'm late."

Janet reached across the desk and caressed my hand. "Look, don't jump to conclusions. Pick up an EPT tonight and make sure before you go getting too worked up over something that may not even be a reality."

"You're right. I don't feel like I am. I mean I haven't had any morning sickness or fatigue," I said still trying to convince myself.

The phones were ringing. Janet stood up, "You gonna be okay?"

"Yes, I'll be fine. Thanks again for helping me get through that."

"Get some rest before interviews and we'll talk later," she said as she walked towards the office door. She then turned around and said, "Natalie, I'm here for you if you need to talk, okay?"

"Thank you, I appreciate that."

She was gone and I was left in my office to think about the distinct possibility, I may be pregnant. I stood up and looked down at my flat stomach and gently rubbed it in disbelief that the product of Kevin's love could be existing in my belly. I wasn't ready for a child, but I loved him. This would not be easy.

Chapter Sixteen

Staying on task was difficult the remainder of the day. I started to ask Janet to run to the drug store on a few occasions to end the suspense. I decided against it, knowing if the test were positive, I wouldn't be any good for the rest of the day and I had to concentrate.

After work, I stopped by Wal-greens. I felt a little embarrassed being seen looking at all the different brands of pregnancy tests. I quickly scanned my options and found an EPT. I picked it up and positioned it in my basket under a roll of toilet paper and the newest issue of Essence magazine. As I watched the line of patrons get smaller, I made my way to the cashier. The teenage girl made eye contact with me when she scanned the test and then gave me my total. I wanted to say, "What the hell are you looking at?" but I played it cool. This was so embarrassing.

I made it home and quickly went into my bathroom and unwrapped the package. After reading the directions, I took the test, being as careful as possible not to mess it up. I laid the flat, narrow device down by the sink and tried to keep myself busy for the next five minutes. I was fidgety. I didn't know what to do so I went to the phone and looked at my caller ID to see who had called. I had missed a call from my parents and Kevin, great, a reminder that two households would be rocked if the test came back positive. It just had to be negative. I looked at my watch — two more minutes. I went to my bedroom to lie on the bed. Trying to be calm, I realized the only thing left to do was say a quick prayer. I prayed that if the Lord revealed to me I wasn't pregnant, I would give up sex until I was married. I then asked for the strength and courage I needed to get through this. I took a deep breath, stood to my feet, and slowly walked in the bathroom. I needed to see one red line, not two. As a approached the sink I closed my eyes, took three deep breaths and slowly opened my eyes to see two red lines staring at me.

My eyes burned and I took a deep breath and swallowed to hold back the tears. I'm pregnant. In disbelief, I unbuttoned my blouse to take a close look at my stomach. Inside me was a baby, a child that I wanted, but not like this. I wasn't married and my boyfriend was a pastor. I could not even think about how to tell Kevin. I was sure he'd be shocked, but I hoped he wouldn't be angry. What would he say? What would he do? I knew he loved me, but did he love me enough to marry me? Did I even want a marriage initiated by the fact I was pregnant?

No matter what answers I came up with, no one will be happy with the end results. My parents always drilled in me the importance of not getting pregnant. They seemed to think that a woman with kids would be viewed less favorably than one without. My mom always said that it would be harder to find a man if you had a child because not too many men would be willing to raise another man's baby. If I did find a man who didn't mind the fact I had a child, he would always view that child differently than any I might have with him. No children equals less baggage.

Kevin would immediately be angry about the whole situation, given his position and his history with already having a child out of wedlock. Although I didn't think he'd want me to have an abortion for religious reasons, he wouldn't be happy on how this would complicate his life.

My mind went back and forth on how to handle this situation. I could choose not to disclose the pregnancy to anyone and just have an abortion. No one would know any different and there would be no drama, hurt feelings or disappointments. But he had the right to know. There's no way I could tackle that tonight. I needed a few days to find the words to tell him.

I didn't bother to return Kevin's call, but I did call home. My parents always worried if I didn't call them back the same day they called me. I tried to put on my most upbeat voice and dialed the number.

"Hello."

"Hi, Momma."

"What's going on, Natalie?"

"Not much, I saw you guys called me, what's going on?" I asked, not being in the mood for conversation."

"I had to take your daddy to the hospital today."

"What?" My heart felt like it was going to jump out of my chest. "What happened?" Desperately needing to know what the situation was, I snapped my questions to my mother.

"He was complaining about his chest feeling tight and he said he was a little dizzy, so I drove him to the VA." She sounded tired.

"Is he okay? Where is he? Is he still in the hospital?"

"He's in there asleep. The doctors changed his heart medication. They said with his condition, it's normal to be a little light headed at times, but there shouldn't be any tightness. They ran some tests, but his heart seems the same, no better or worse."

I sat down on my couch to gain my composure. The thought of anything happening to my dad terrified me. "If he's sleep, definitely don't wake him, but tell him I called when he wakes up. What brought this on?" I asked needing to know the root of what could have triggered it.

My mother went on to say that my father had been doing okay. She said she was going to call her office to inform them she was going to take a leave of absence, so she could be at home to monitor his condition better. That made me feel better.

"I'm going to make arrangements to come home within the week for a few days. Tell Daddy to call me tomorrow, okay?"

"Okay, goodnight."

"Bye."

For a moment I forgot about my problem and focused on a much larger one. My dad meant the world to me and I had to see him, if for no other reason, but to make him feel better.

Chapter Seventeen

A couple of days and several conversations had passed without me mentioning a word about the pregnancy. I knew I had to bring it up tonight, just to get everything out in the open. I was nervous thinking about his reaction. I expected him to be angry, but I was unsure how he would act out his anger. I hoped he wouldn't blame me or look at me differently, but realize our love could get us through this.

It was after ten o'clock when I heard the phone ring.

"Hello?"

"Hey, what are you doing?" Kevin asked sounding a little tired, but still in a good mood.

"I'm good. How was Bible study?"

"It was good. We had a lot of people in attendance tonight. Good service."

"That's good," I paused not knowing how to bring up the news. I was so jittery. "Kevin?"

"Yeah, Babe."

"Where are you?"

"I'm on my couch. Why? What's up?" He asked with concern in his voice, sensing the vibe.

"I don't know how to say this…" I said trying to find the words, "but I'm pregnant." I swallowed to moisten my throat. My heart raced and the silence on the other end of the phone tortured me. For a few seconds, I couldn't tell if anyone was even on the line. I was scared to say anything. I finally mustered up the courage to say "Kevin, you there?"

"Yeah, I'm here." He said in a very dry voice. He didn't sound like the same man.

"Did you hear me?"

I heard a deep inhale, followed by a long exhale. "I heard you Natalie. But, how did this happen? I mean I was so careful."

"You know pulling out is not the greatest form of birth control. We both knew that." There was silence again. I wish I could see his face, but actually I didn't want to face the disappointment.

He was silent for about ten seconds then he burst out with, "I just don't understand." His voice was fading. "Lord, God. How could this happen?" He sounded hurt and angry.

I didn't know how to respond. "Listen, I'm sorry. But it is true."

"I don't doubt that, Natalie. I should've known better. I knew I was potent, but..." His voice faded away again to the point where I could not comprehend what he was saying. Then there was silence. "So, what now?" he asked in a dry, unsympathetic voice.

"What do you mean 'what now'?" Tears were filling my eyes. I couldn't believe how cold his tone was. I understood he was hurt, but it wasn't entirely my fault.

"What are you gonna do about this? Have you thought about it?" he asked, sounding emotionally detached from the question.

"I thought we could discuss it. I realize there are options, but either decision would be a difficult one." Tears had started to fall.

I heard him take a deep breath. "Listen, I'm not going to tell you what to do about this. Ultimately, it doesn't matter how I feel about the situation, the decision is yours."

Although I didn't want him to notice I was crying, I could no longer hold back the tears. "You are putting the weight of this whole situation on my shoulders, which isn't fair. We have to talk about it, Kevin. There is another life to consider. And you do have a say in this. I need to know how you feel."

"Natalie, I love you and I trust you will make the best decision for everybody," he said in a low calm voice.

Our conversation had brought me no answers I wanted to hear. If he truly wanted this baby, he would have said so. I was not prepared to be a mother, but at least I was willing to talk about it. Without actually saying it, he wanted no part of being a father and I didn't want to be a mother to a child who was unwanted by his father. I could not and would not allow this "mistake" to ruin the promise of our future. Abortion was now the only option.

After the next morning's meeting, I made an appointment to go to the clinic to have an abortion. Amazingly, they had an opening the next day, which I promptly accepted. The next availability would be in a week and I didn't want to wait that long. I felt the longer I waited, the harder it would be. When I talked to Kevin about my decision, he had very little to say other than he had a funeral the day of my termination and would be unable to fly down to be by my side during the procedure.

By lunchtime, Janet came in and asked me how I was feeling. I had already confided in her about my decision and she didn't judge or try to convince me otherwise.

"How's the interview lineup today?" I asked as I shuffled through a small pile of papers on my desk.

"We have a few, maybe four. The phones have been pretty light today. As a matter of fact, I haven't scheduled any for tomorrow."

That triggered a memory and I told her that I had my procedure scheduled for tomorrow at eleven and for her not to schedule anything for the whole day. Then I came to the realization that life must still go on and I instructed for her to schedule as many interviews as she could and Christopher could do them.

"Are you scared?" She asked as she walked closer to my desk and took a seat.

"Terrified is more like it," I said making eye contact with her.

"You'll be okay. What time is Kevin flying in?"

"He's not. He has a funeral tomorrow," I said, trying hard to sound unaffected by the fact he would be a no show.

"He's what?! He's not coming?" she said in a loud, aggravated tone. "That motherfucker got you pregnant and he doesn't even have the decency to fly his ass down here to be by your side during one of the most difficult times of your life?" she said all in one breath, without batting an eye. Normally, she would at least try to respond in a more politically correct fashion when addressing me, but this time she didn't hold back.

"I'm not crazy about the idea of going through this by myself, but I don't have a choice. He's a preacher and he has a pastoral duty to tend to."

"Natalie, stop taking up for him. What about his duty and responsibility to you?"

She was right on. So right, I didn't even mind her tone of voice or directness. Everything she was saying I had thought, but what could I do? Demand he fly down, cancel a funeral engagement, drop everything at a drop of a hat because I couldn't wait a week to make an appointment? No, this was my mess and I had to handle it in the best way and time I saw fit.

"Janet, I appreciate your concern. It truly touches me that you care enough to say the things you have. But, this is how it is. I'll be okay." I tried hard to give her the most reassuring smile as I could.

"Do you want me to drive you?"

"No, I can manage. The lady at the clinic said depending on the type of termination I choose the recovery time would be short and I could drive myself home, if needed. I should be okay." I reached across the desk and squeezed the yellow, manicured hand that had extended help and comfort when I needed it.

"Okay, but the offer stands." She paused. "You okay? You want something to eat?" she asked as she stood and collected the documents I had arranged for her to file.

"No, I don't have much of an appetite." I didn't want to tell her that the thought of food made me feel sicker than I already felt.

Chapter Eighteen

I woke up the next morning having mixed feelings of fear, confusion, and regret. I had never had an abortion and I never thought I would. I feared I was making the wrong decision. I could be terminating the life of the next Nobel Peace Prize Winner or a famous brain surgeon. I was confused that a year from now I would regret having ever chosen this route, but for now there was no other choice. I had to make peace with the decision. There was no other way.

After my bath, I chose a casual denim dress. It would be easy to maneuver, given the circumstances. On my way to the clinic, I called Janet on my cell to touch base. She said Christopher seemed to have everything under control and everyone was preparing to go out in the field. I had instructed Janet to tell everyone I was conducting a training at another office and would be unavailable during the day. The last few minutes of our conversation consisted of me giving her a list of things for Christopher to do and a list of her own. She ended our call by telling me she was praying for me and if I needed a ride from the clinic, don't hesitate to call.

My heart beat faster as I pulled into the parking lot of the unidentifiable building. The only way I knew this building was the one I was looking for was because I had driven by twice and seen the address of the two buildings surrounding the unidentifiable one and figured it had to be the place.

As I stepped off the elevator and approached Suite 232, I took a deep breath. I opened the door to see a room full of women. I guess unplanned or unwanted pregnancies are not unique to a particular class, creed or color. I walked to the counter and was given a clipboard with forms I needed to fill out. I found a seat between a girl that looked about fifteen and a young couple. Twenty minutes later, I returned the paper work to the heavy set Hispanic lady at the counter and returned to my seat and patiently waited.

Sitting there, I looked in the faces of the many women and wondered what situations brought them to their decision to terminate their pregnancies. There were several young girls who were accompanied by their parents, a few women in their twenties and thirties, and a handful of couples. Looking deeply in the eyes of the women, it was evident that there were so many stories in this room, but I couldn't imagine any more heart breaking than my own. I closed my eyes and tried to settle my nerves and wait for the conclusion of this bad dream.

About thirty agonizing minutes later, my name was called. I nervously got up and walked in the examination room. A different nurse came and collected a urine sample and directed me to a room where I was given a paper robe to put on while they gave me an ultrasound. I lay on the table and was taken off guard by the cold gel the nurse applied to my abdomen while she moved a flat device over it. She pressed a few buttons and informed me I was thirty-two days pregnant. That would put conception date around the R&R Weekend. Kevin and I had made love several times in the Bahamas and all without a condom.

I was taken to yet another room where I sat for a few minutes with only my regrets and fears to keep me company. An older black man who came through the door interrupted my thoughts. "Ms. Thomas," he said as he extended his hand. "I'm Dr. Matthews. "

The middle-aged man reminded me of my dad. I looked down quickly, embarrassed by my condition and then raised my head enough to say, "Hello."

The handsome older gentleman scanned his chart and said, "Well, it looks like we are a little over four weeks pregnant." He looked up from his chart and over his small framed glasses and asked, "Is this your first abortion?"

"Yes, sir."

"Well then, I'm going to need you to scoot your bottom to the end of the table and put your feet in the stirrups."

I felt like crawling under the table. Not only was this fatherly man going to administer my abortion, but also I bet he was thinking I was some whore. I wanted to tell him I was responsible, that I didn't sleep around, and that at this very moment, I wish I could die.

He pushed his hand gently on three or four spots on my stomach, while he attempted to explain what I would experience. "I'm going to insert these clamps at the opening of your vagina," he said as he raised them so I could see. "Then you are going to experience some discomfort, but it won't be for long, just try your best to relax your legs during the process. Afterwards, you will hear something that sounds like a vacuum and a pulling sensation. Then you'll be all done. Shall we begin?"

I nodded my agreement and lay my head on the small pillow and closed my eyes. I braced myself as I heard the clacking of the clamps then the coldness on my skin as it made contact. There was discomfort, but it was bearable. I then let out a small scream as I felt what felt like several small knives or needles enter me.

"Relax, Ms. Thomas. It won't hurt as much if you relax."

I gritted my teeth and tried to focus my attention on the door. The pain was agonizing; I barely noticed a female nurse had entered the room. The scraping felt deep and piercing. I did everything not to cry. There was a pause in the pressure and pain, then I felt a different device that must have been that vacuum he warned me about begin to torture me with more scraping joined by a pulling agony. Unable to keep still, I moved my head from side to side as I bit my lip to hold back the scream that lay so close to the surface. It felt like he was destroying all of what was inside me and actually he was. Then it was silent. It was over and tears that tried so hard to escape earlier could no longer be contained and made footprints down my face.

I felt feverish all over as the nurse guided me to the recovery room where four other women were recovering. I needed to sit down or I would faint. I suppose the nurse could see it because her grip tightened around my arm. She sat me down on a couch next to an attractive white woman who I believe was in her early thirties. Her eyes were red as she sat bent over her knees. I was handed three cookies and a glass of orange juice. After about twenty minutes, my feverish dizziness had subsided enough for me to leave. I was handed a prescription of painkillers and exited the recovery room.

The attractive white lady I was seated near in the recovery room was greeted with a kiss and hug by a man who I assumed was her boyfriend. I was faced with the reality that there were no hugs, kisses or TLC from Kevin awaiting me, only a long drive home — alone. I had never felt more alone and depressed. On the elevator, I burst into tears filled with confusion and disbelief not only for what I had just experienced, but the fact that the man I loved was not here to wipe away my tears. As the elevator opened, someone who had not forgotten about me immediately embraced me. Someone who somehow knew the emotional and physical pain I would be experiencing, someone who refused to let me go through it alone. Janet, my receptionist, took my keys from my hand and drove me home.

Janet stayed with me that night, coming in my room from time to time to give me some apple juice, a snack, or my prescription Tylenol. I didn't even bother to ask who was running the office, I knew she had probably given Christopher some excuse about an emergency she had to tend to and left him in charge.

My phone rang several times, but she never interrupted my rest. It was probably Kevin and with the way she felt about him, she probably wouldn't give me the phone even if I were up and around. By nightfall, the cramping had subsided a bit, enough for me to walk a little. I changed my huge maxi pad and joined Janet in the living room. She was watching a rerun of *A Different World*.

"How are you feeling?" she asked, directing her attention to me.

"A little better, still cramping though." I said carefully taking a seat on my leather chair.

"Has the medicine helped at all?"

"Yeah. It's helped. Have you spoken to Christopher? How's the office?" I asked needing to know all was well.

"Good. I got off the phone with Christopher a couple of hours ago. He enjoyed having the office to himself today. He said that everyone's numbers were steady and he completed all his paperwork and interviews. Oh, yeah, he added there are two new starts tomorrow," she said with a smile.

"Well, that's good to know that he can handle things totally on his own. I heard the phone ring a few times. Who called?"

"Do you have to ask? Kevin called eight times. He demanded for me to let him talk to you, but I told him you were asleep."

I felt good knowing he cared enough to call so many times and for him to demand for Janet to put me on the phone made me feel even better.

"What did he say?" I asked, needing to know the details.

"He got an attitude, but he'll be okay. He should've been here, then he would've known how you were doing first hand," Janet said with a slight attitude.

I could appreciate Janet's support of me, but there was something in me that made me feel uncomfortable about her bad mouthing Kevin.

The phone rang.

"That's probably him," she said as she smacked her lips. "You want me to get it?"

"No, that's okay, I got it."

I walked in my room, reclined on some pillows on my bed and picked up the phone on my nightstand.

"Hello?"

"Natalie, there you are, are you okay, Baby?" he asked sounding very sincere.

"I'm okay. Still cramping a lot, though." I said attempting to sound worse than I actually felt. He wasn't going to get off that easy. He was going to know about the pain I had experienced. He should at least feel guilty about not consoling me though the recovery process.

"Sweetie, I'm sorry. I see you have Janet there to help you. I'm going to catch a flight out there tomorrow to be with you."

"That won't be necessary. I'm flying to Dallas on Friday. It won't be worth you coming out for just one day. Besides the worst is over."

"How's your dad doing?"

"Not too good. I need to fly out and spend about three or four days with him, so I can see for myself. Listen, the pain killer is kicking in and I'm getting sleepy," I said, not really wanting to get off the phone, but I needed to draw first blood and end the call.

He hesitated and said, "I love you Natalie. I'll call you in the morning to check on you."

"Okay, I love you, too. Bye, bye." I was upset at the fact that I had weakened to the point of saying I love you, but it was true, despite it all.

Chapter Nineteen

I walked out of the terminal and was faced with the realization that the reception I had received in the past was no longer. I searched the many unfamiliar faces, not to find my daddy's. Maybe I should be looking for my mother or sister, but they were missing as well. I blamed it on the traffic and waited thirty minutes, then decided to check my cell phone's voice mail.

"Nat, this is Veronica. Daddy was rushed to the emergency room and Donna will be picking you up outside the baggage claim." My sister's words hit me like a train. I sprinted through the double doors that opened to the small crowd of smokers waiting for cabs. A few minutes later, I saw my cousin's Blazer approaching and I hurried through the people to the curb and flagged her down by waving both hands. So much time had been wasted.

"Hey, Natalie," Donna said as she quickly got out of the driver's side long enough to give me a quick hug and open the trunk to put my bag in. Donna's long, thick hair was in a ponytail and she was wearing sweat pants and a t-shirt. Judging from her appearance and facial expression, she was rushed and was totally aware of the urgency of the moment.

"Is everything okay? What happened?" I asked trying my best to get all the details.

"All I know is that your sister called me a couple of hours ago and told me your dad had passed out and the ambulance was taking him to St. Paul." I could tell she was making an effort not to sound scared. "What took you so long? Was your flight late? I've been circling around for the past half hour?"

"I just got Veronica's message. Please hurry, Donna. If anything has happened to him..." I began to cry, overwhelmed by the uncertainty.

An hour later we ran through the automatic doors to the Emergency Room. I immediately saw my mother and sister seated on the chairs talking to someone I assumed to be the nurse. My mother and sister looked up long enough to see us run in, but their attention quickly returned to the nurse.

"What's going on? Is he okay?" I asked quickly, wanting an answer just as quick.

There was a moment of silence, then my sister said, "This morning he had another heart attack, Nat." My heart raced and uncontrollable tears did not hesitate to make an appearance. "He's stable now, but the doctors want to keep him a few days."

"I want to see him," I said looking at the nurse and speaking with more authority than I had heard from myself in months. I was angry at the fact that a man that was so spirit filled, so loving, so loved, and so kind had to suffer like this. It wasn't fair and I needed to see him to let him know that I was there.

"He's sedated, Natalie," my mother said in a very tired and low voice.

Irritated, I stood up and said, " What does that mean? Is he in some type of a coma?"

The nurse interrupted by saying, "Ms. Thomas, calm down and have a seat." Her voice was calming. "Your dad is not in a coma. We gave him some medication so he can get some needed rest. He's been through a lot today. He should be waking up in a few hours and at that time I'm sure he would love to see you."

"Okay, okay," I repeated slowly, trying to get under control. "Thanks, nurse. But ..." I paused realizing I might not want to know the answer to the question I needed to ask, "Is he going to be okay?" My voice trembled with fear as I braced myself for the answer.

"Your dad seems to be a strong man. I'm not the doctor, but I can tell you his vitals are stable and this attack did not seem to do any major damage. He was very fortunate to get to the hospital when he did."

I immediately called Kevin to catch him up on what was going on. I'd called him on the way to the hospital and he said he was going to catch the next flight out to Dallas as soon as I called him with my dad's condition. The sympathetic tone of his voice and comforting words calmed me. He realized I had a rough 48 hours and he needed to be by my side. He would be taking the eight AM flight out of Chicago Midway tomorrow and would be in Dallas Love Field at ten forty. I was touched he had taken the liberty to book the flight before actually receiving word on my dad's condition. He prayed for my dad over the phone, told me he loved me and that he would see me in the morning.

I called Janet and Christopher to let them know I would not be returning to the office on Tuesday, but because of what happened I would be in touch. They both offered their prayers and well wishes. Janet told me in her own direct, yet sassy way, "now you take as much time as you need, I'll watch over these fools." That was her special little way to get me to smile. And it did.

Christopher, who was always so upbeat and energetic, told me he was sorry about my dad, but he would be privileged with the opportunity to make me proud by running the show solo. It was funny that they both felt they were the one calling the shots in my absence. Regardless, I knew everything would be okay while I was away.

An hour or so later, the nurse allowed us the opportunity to see my dad. As I slowly opened the door, with my mother and sister following closely behind, I saw the broad figure of the man who had stood so tall and strong all of my life laying flat on his back in the sterile hospital room. He had tubes in his nose and a machine tracking his heart rhythms beside his bed. I noticed an IV disbursing medication in two bags hanging on a tall rack near by. As we walked closer, he opened his eyes making eye contact with us and smiled. I leaned over and kissed his forehead wanting him to feel the love from my lips through his skin. He opened his mouth and tried to say something that was interrupted by a vicious cough.

"Don't try and talk, you need your rest," my mother said in a kind, loving voice.

"Please, don't talk. We'll talk tomorrow," I added.

For a moment, no words were needed. We all just stood there making some type of physical contact with him. I was rubbing one arm, my sister was caressing his legs and my mother was holding his hand. For the first time, in a long while, we were all connected, as one. Unfortunately, it had taken a tragedy to make it happen.

Chapter Twenty

I arrived at the airport just in time to see Kevin's plane approach the gate. I rushed in the ladies restroom to change my maxi-pad I still had to wear from the abortion just three days before. I tucked my t-shirt into my Levis shorts and tightened my ponytail. All in all, I wasn't dressed to kill nor was my makeup immaculate, but I was presentable. This time Kevin was not the main attraction of the day.

He stepped off the plane dressed in a blue suit and white shirt, with no tie, looking fine as ever. He immediately saw me standing nearby. He didn't smile, but walked over to me and gave me the most endearing hug that he knew I needed.

The ride to the hospital was a quiet one. I told him everything the doctor and nurse had told me. During my effort to explain, he held my hand and would bring it up to his lips to kiss it from time to time. Assistant Pastor Henderson would be conducting Sunday morning service and handling all other responsibilities until Kevin's return.

I had filled my sister and mother in on Kevin the night before. I only told them I was dating a preacher who lived in Chicago, but nothing else. They didn't need to know about the daughter he had, nor the possible son or daughter that once was. I knew they would take to him. He had the type of personality and look that most people would be drawn to.

We walked into the hospital and immediately saw my mother, sister and brother-in-law seated in the waiting room. We rushed over. "Have you seen him? Is he okay?" I asked.

"Yes, he seems to be doing much better. We haven't spoken to the doctor this morning, but we saw him and he's sitting up and trying to talk," my sister said, happily smiling from ear to ear.

"Praise God, thank you Jesus," I screamed as I hugged her releasing all the anxiety in my body. I then noticed everyone's eyes directed to Kevin.

"I'm so sorry. Kevin this is my mother, Mrs. Thomas, sister, Veronica, and brother-in-law, Lance," I said as I pointed to each.

Kevin said his hellos and shook everyone's hand, then excused himself to the men's room. As soon as he was out of sight, my sister and mother looked at me simultaneously with a look of shock and disbelief.

"My goodness, Natalie. Umph, I don't know what to say about that one," my mother said, smiling while shaking her hand.

My sister just looked dumbfounded.

"He's like a black John F. Kennedy, Jr." my mother added.

For the next two minutes, I was swarmed with questions about his age, his education, his height, how long I'd known him, and his degree of involvement with me. Amazingly enough, I was honest with every question, I figured with our relationship growing closer by the day, there was no need to hide anything at this point.

I was just explaining how we met when he emerged from the restroom. He walked directly towards me and kissed my forehead.

"Mrs. Thomas, have you eaten? I would be happy to run and get something for everyone to eat," Kevin said.

"Thank you so much for asking." She looked at my sister and brother-in-law as if to see how they were holding up. "Well, I think we could all go for a sandwich or something," she said as she turned towards the chair where her purse was resting.

"By all means, it's my treat. Is Subway okay? I think we passed one right up the street, didn't we, Nat?" The next few minutes were filled with me writing down everyone's sandwich orders. I gave Kevin my car keys and sheet of paper of three sandwich requests and off he went.

I walked to the hospital room and looked through the glass window to see my dad's weak frame lying on the bed. He appeared to be asleep. I asked a nurse, who was walking by, if I could go in. After reviewing his chart she said it was okay. I slowly opened the door and quietly walked in, confused on whether to let him sleep or wake him. I needed to hear him say he was okay. I needed him to know I was by his side.

I stood there just looking at him, trying to mentally engrave every facial feature in my brain. A few minutes went by before I saw his eyes slowly flutter, then open. He smiled. My heart warmed.

"Hey, Natalie. When did you get here?" He seemed to struggle to get the words out. His voice sounded raspy and hoarse.

"I just walked in. How are you doing? Are you in any pain?"

He shook his head from side to side to indicate that he was okay and pain-free. "Naw, they have me too drugged up to be in any pain." He giggled. "I feel fine, now. I'm glad to see you."

My dad always had a positive attitude and it was just like him to make jokes in a situation like this. I'm sure he was trying to make me feel better and he did. I heard the door open to find a nurse had come in. She quietly told me I needed to prepare to leave so he could get some rest.

I searched for the words to express my feelings for him. I wanted to tell him I loved him. Those words had never come out of my mouth before towards any of my family. We never said it, even though it was understood we were loved. It wasn't until Cindy and Sandy started ending their phone calls with "I love you" about a year ago, when I started telling them. I tell Kevin, so I definitely should tell my dad.

"The nurse is kicking me out. Get some rest." I bent down to give him a long hug, and then I kissed his cheek and whispered, "I love you" in his ear. As I was leaving, I glanced back at my father only to find tears in his eyes matching the tears in mine.

I left the room feeling empowered by the fact that he was going to be okay. I felt a sense of freedom from the shackles of not being able to tell him I loved him. It took twenty-seven years, but I was free and I felt awesome knowing that during his most trying time not only was I sure he felt I loved him, but he heard the words I had never spoken to him.

In the waiting room, Kevin had returned from Subway. Everyone was talking, eating, and smiling. Kevin stood up when he noticed I had entered the room and returned the smile I had on my face when I saw everyone.

"How's he doing?" Veronica asked, chewing her tuna sub.

"He's doing good. Really good. He's gonna be okay." I believed every word.

Chapter Twenty-One

"How many interviews do we have today, Janet?" I called out from my office into the lobby. I was disturbed by the fact we had recently lost five people and I needed to rebuild.

"We have seven."

"That's it!! Did ya'll place the ad in the paper?" I screamed into the lobby.

Janet appeared at my door. "Yes, ads were run, but the phones just aren't ringing that much," she said in her own defense.

"Try your best to book every call in for an interview and bring me a copy of the ads you guys ran as soon as possible. Something's wrong. We have a few new promotions coming and we need as many qualified people on the books to handle the load." I said trying to communicate the importance of the situation.

Moments later, after she fulfilled my requests and sensed I had calmed down, Janet appeared at my door. "Are you okay? How was your trip? Is your dad okay?"

"I'm fine. My dad is doing a lot better. He's back at home."

"Praise God. I was praying for him." She said as she walked in and sat down at my desk.

"How's Kevin?"

"Kevin is great. He actually flew down to be with my family and me. He was truly a God send," I responded by keeping my attention on the report displayed on my computer.

"How long did he stay?"

"He flew in the day after I arrived and he left the same morning I did to return to Chicago."

She smiled and said, "That was nice."

"As a matter of fact, I need to go to the mall to pick up an outfit for Skyler."

"Skyler, who is that?" Janet inquired.

"Skyler, I told you. His daughter, remember?" It was so hard to keep an employee/employer relationship with Janet. Over time I had confided a lot of personal things to her, which made it difficult to treat her like a paid worker. But, I wouldn't have it any other way.

"That's right. So, you're finally going to meet her," she said with a hint of an "about damn time" tone.

"Yes, Kevin was finally able to arrange a meeting. We will both spend the weekend in Indianapolis. He's coming here tomorrow and we will fly there together."

"You know, whenever I start to doubt this man's motives he goes and does something sweet like flying to Dallas to be with you and your family and scheduling a meeting with his daughter. He might be all right, Natalie."

"Told ya. He is damn near perfect," I said enthusiastically.

"So, can you see yourself being a First Lady?"

That was a question I had pondered for months now. It was a very good possibility that Kevin would ask me to marry him. All the signs were there. He tells me he loves me daily, had invested the time and money to visit me, we traveled together, he was there during my dad's hospital stay, and I was about to meet his child. Just because he wasn't ready to be a dad, doesn't mean he's not ready to get married. The writing was definitely on the wall.

"I'm sure it would be an adjustment, but I love him and I love the Lord," I said trying to sound confident. "I know I need more knowledge about the Bible, but I'm saved. With time, I'm sure I'll be able to fit right into the role."

"You need to think about this long and hard, Natalie. As a First Lady you are far more than the pastor's wife. It's a huge responsibility. Biblically, you need to be prepared to cover your husband in prayer in the midnight hours when he comes under attack and be a pillar of strength when he and the church need it. You will be ministering to the women of the church and leading several ministries and organizations," she paused. "Look, I know you are a powerful black woman. You are successful, educated, articulate, knowledgeable, bright and beautiful, but if you honestly think that your relationship is headed towards marriage you need to position yourself to grow more in the scripture and your relationship with God."

I didn't quite know how to take what I was hearing. Was Janet saying that I wasn't good enough to be a First Lady? "Janet, if there's one thing I know about myself it's that I'm one of the most kind-hearted people out there. I'm giving and sincere. There's not a day that goes by that I don't give a needy person a dollar or loan out company money to someone in the office that's in a bind. It saddens me to think that you don't think I can be a First Lady," I said in my own defense. "I know I'm not perfect, but I am saved and I love the Lord. I know I need growth, but isn't everyone going through growth?"

"Yes, Sweetie, but this is different. You are one of the kindest people I have ever known, but I'm just saying," she took a deep breath as if she were searching for the right words, "you have to continuously seek God and live the life he would want you to live. And excuse me for saying this, but it doesn't help that you are fornicating with the pastor."

This hit me like a ton of bricks, but she was right. I needed to get back on the spiritual track I had been on all my life. Since moving to New York I had visited a few churches, but had not joined any. I blamed it on the fact that I wasn't being spiritually fed, and I wasn't. I needed to seek God for me, not for Kevin.

"Natalie, I'm sorry if I was out of line, but I just want you to know what you will be faced with, if it goes there," Janet stated.

"I know Janet. I can't lie that it was easy to hear, but you are right."

By the end of the day, I had completed eight interviews, scheduled five for a second interview, called my dad, signed off on the sales, and prepared for tomorrow morning's meeting.

The sales were steady, given the fact it had rained. Nevertheless, everyone was in a good mood and that was the most important thing. After work, I stopped by the mall and found the cutest little pastel colored outfit for Skyler. I picked out a size 36 months. Even though she's two, I wanted to make sure it fit.

"Would you like it gift-wrapped?" the teenager asked.

"No, thank you. I'll take it as it is." I wanted to show the outfit to Kevin to get his opinion. I couldn't wait for him to see it. It was very important for him to know that I embrace his daughter and I look forward to a relationship with her. Just like the first outfit I bought a few months ago, this outfit was also a symbol of that.

Chapter Twenty-Two

I was awakened by the sultry sound of *Sweet Love* by Anita Baker. I looked at the clock and saw the red numbers indicating it was 6:15 AM. Pulling the pillow over my head, I snuggled my body in the sheets with an attempt to get fifteen more minutes, then decided to get up, realizing the hectic day I had in store for me.

Half asleep, I walked into my bathroom and started the shower and slugged back into the bedroom to turn up the radio to listen to the Tom Joyner Morning Show. What was I to wear today? I opened my closet to find a very feminine pink suit my mother had recently sent me and that Kevin had not seen me in. This would be cute.

After my shower, I styled my hair in a classy up sweep, dressed, applied my makeup, grabbed my gift for Skyler to show Kevin and was out the door, all in forty-five minutes. The ride to the office was filled with thoughts of any office duties for the day and fitting in the time to swing to the airport to pick up Kevin. I figured I could always get Janet or Christopher to step in, if I needed to.

The next couple of days would be momentous. I would be meeting the most important person in Kevin's life. I wasn't pleased with the fact that he had already experienced the birth of a child with another woman, but I had grown to accept it. Amazingly enough, the fact that he conceived a child out of wedlock had become insignificant. I knew that he had fallen short of the grace of God, as all people do and he is a man with desires that he had succumbed to.

It was a beautiful day, which typically meant good sales. People would be in a good mood, which would make them more receptive to my salespeople. I stopped by Dunkin Donuts and picked up four-dozen glazed donuts. I did this from time to time, to break the morning routine of the guys coming in, choosing a territory, conducting practice pitching, running a meeting, and going to the field. Even though all of that would still go on, at least the sugar from the donuts would put them in a happier mood and on a higher energy level. The meeting was good and as I predicted, the guys were hyped and motivated to have a great sales day. Returning to my desk, I saw a message from my accountant. I called her back, apparently she needed me to approve the payroll, bills to be paid this week and figures for the checks for the guys in the office. After all was said and done, my company's bank balance was still a little over $107,000. I was floating on air. I was so blessed to have a successful business, a loving family, and a fine, Christian man. God is good — all the time.

Kevin's flight was running twenty minutes late, which afforded me needed primp time in the airport restroom. I sprayed a few squirts of my Paloma Picasso perfume on my neck, wrist and suit jacket. After over seven months of dating, looking good to him was still very important to me. I still carefully chose every outfit and styled my hair in the most flattering styles. I needed for him to desire my mind, spirit and body.

Before he saw me, I spotted him looking like a model on GQ Magazine. I shuffled trying to stand in the most attractive stance. He was still able to bring out that uneasy little girl feeling when I was around him. He made eye contact with me and walked over, smiling slightly, but oh so sexy.

"How are you?"

"Good. You?"

"I'm good, you look beautiful."

"Thank you. Is this all you have?" I asked motioning toward his blue carry on.

"Yeah, it is," he answered seeming a bit preoccupied.

In the car, he was quiet. I tried to spark up some conversation, but he didn't elaborate much. Remembering, the gift for Skyler I had in the back seat, I reached back to get in when his cell phone rang.

He glanced at his Caller ID and took a deep breath.

"Yes," he answered sharply. He was obviously disturbed with whoever was on the other line. I just drove and listened.

"I sent the money Western Union. It's there. Check again." He looked in his pocket and pulled out what must have been the Western Union receipt. "Look, I sent the amount you said you needed. I got to go. I'll be there in the morning." He pressed the end button on the phone without saying goodbye.

Curious, I asked, "What was that about?"

"That was Shelby. She blew two tires and called me pleading for some money."

All of a sudden, I felt angry. Why was it his responsibility to make sure she had tires? They weren't together. His responsibility was for that child, not the mom.

"Why is she calling you for that?"

"Apparently, she needed it. She said she didn't have it."

"Okay, but Kevin, it is not your responsibility to tend to her every need." It angered me knowing any time this woman had a need he jumped.

He was quiet. Then all of a sudden he said angrily, "Listen, I know I shouldn't have to do it, but Skyler rides in that car to go to daycare and just for safety's sake I have to look out for my child."

"Are those your words or hers?" I said coldly.

"I'm not going to have you dictate what I do for my child," he replied sternly.

"Kevin, I'm not the one dictating. Your baby's momma is doing a great job at that. Are you still sleeping with her?" I responded furiously without even thinking.

"Hell, no, I can't stand the bitch! I don't like the fact I had to do it. I shouldn't have to," he yelled back to me, rubbing his temples.

I had never heard Kevin so mad and cursing, at that. I didn't know how to respond. I had so much to say, but I didn't want to make matters worse. Apparently, this was what I had detected being on his mind prior to the call.

The car was quiet and the mood was tense until we pulled into the parking lot of the office. I was relieved to have reached a location that could allow me to have some space away from him.

Walking in the office, there were two people seated in the lobby waiting for an interview.

"Hello, Mr. Lewis," Janet said politely, looking up from her paperwork. "Natalie, I put your messages on your desk."

The next hour was filled with me conducting interviews and returning phone calls. I had no idea of Kevin's whereabouts until I found him in a back office talking on his cell phone. I didn't want to appear as though I was trying to be in his business, so I left. Before, I could turn the corner I heard, "Natalie, wait, come back." I pretended like I didn't hear the request and kept walking. After all, I just wanted to know where he was; I didn't want to talk until I knew how I truly felt about the baby momma drama that had now presented itself.

As we arrived at my apartment complex, I realized I had not shown Kevin the gift for Skyler. After getting out of the car, I reached in the back seat and retrieved my purse and her pink gift bag and noticed Kevin had already made it to my apartment door. Reaching him, I unlocked the door and we both walked into the living room.

"You want something to drink?" I asked dryly.

"No, I'm okay. What's that in the bag?" He pointed to the pink gift bag I still had in my hand.

I walked over and handed Skyler's present to him and walked to the kitchen. "It's a little something I picked up for Skyler. I saw it and had to get it. I think it will look adorable on her."

Kevin's eyes brightened. "You didn't have to do that. Come here." He stood there looking so sincere, so sexy. My heart weakened as I approached him to find my familiar spot between his arms. All of a sudden, all anger was gone.

He sat on my couch and pulled out the pink and white tissue paper that covered the outfit I had carefully chosen. Smiling from ear to ear he said, "Natalie, this is so nice of you to have done. She will love it."

"I just wanted to give her something when I see her tomorrow. When I saw it, I knew it would be perfect for her. You don't think it's too big, do you?" I stood there, elated at the fact that he liked it.

All of a sudden he was quiet again. "Sit down, Natalie. Something's come up."

Still standing, I said, "What, what's the matter?" Bracing myself for the unknown.

"Shelby is not ready for Skyler to be exposed to any 'girlfriend' of mine. As a matter of fact, she went far enough to say that if I show up with someone, she would not allow me to see Skyler."

"You've got to be kidding me!" I couldn't believe this woman could be so controlling.

"No, unfortunately, I'm not." He said softly, looking downward.

"I don't believe this. I don't understand why she would react this way, unless you just sprung it on her. Does she even know about me?"

"Yes, of course she does. I think it's just reality setting in, plus she is just very protective of Skyler. She's her whole world."

I interrupted, "And she's using Skyler in every way possible to control you. First, with making you feel guilty so you can buy her tires for her car and now with trying to dictate who she wants to expose your child to." Starting to tremble I added, "I don't like this, I don't like this at all."

"Damn it, Natalie. I don't either. But, it's not my fault!"

I walked into the kitchen not wanting Kevin to see my tears from not being able to control my emotions.

I screamed out into the living room, "You know, I'm beginning to wonder where the blame lies," pausing to blow a running nose. "She is controlling you because you are allowing it."

Joining me in the kitchen, he was now inches away. "What the hell is that supposed to mean?" His energy and closeness made me uneasy.

"Kevin, you are paying child support, aren't you?"

"Of course."

"Then you have rights, rights that she cannot withhold from you. Hell, take her ass to court!"

"It's not that type of arrangement, Nat."

"What type of arrangement is it? You pay child support, so the courts are on your side."

He took a deep breath. "Our arrangement is not through the courts."

"What does that mean?" I had little to no knowledge about child support issues.

"We came up with the amount I would pay and the visitation."

"Okay, so what are the terms of your agreement?"

"I pay $1,000 a month and I can see her once a month.

I felt blood rush to my face. "You mean you pay that woman a thousand dollars a month for a two year old child that you are only allowed to see once a month!" I paused to get a hold on myself. "I don't know much about babies, but I know diapers and formula can't add up to that much. Besides, she should be able to buy her own damn tires with $1,000. Can't you see she's taking advantage of you?"

Kevin walked away from me and turned back and said, "I don't appreciate your telling me how much is too much support in regards to my child. Truth be told, I wish I could give more."

Not being able to take any more of the conversation, I walked past him, deliberately bumping his shoulder, into my bedroom and slammed the door where I got on my bed and sobbed uncontrollably. He could not see how she was taking him to the bank, knowing he would be too ashamed to stand in front of a judge, reveal he was a preacher, and further expose this situation in future legal documents for anyone to have public access to. The part that hurt most was it was like he was taking her side.

The creak of my bedroom door and footsteps walking towards me awakened me about an hour later. My body stiffened when I felt the pressure of his body sit on the edge of the bed. I lay still, acting as if I were asleep. I felt his hand run down my back down to my butt where he caressed the round curve.

"Natalie?" His voice was very deep and broken.

I did not move or say a word. I felt empty and stripped of the future life I had longed for with him.

"Natalie, please wake up." His voice was muffled with sounds of misery. He was weeping gently and I could no longer deny him the comfort he needed from me. I slowly rose and in the dark of the room I could see the wetness of his eyes and the trail of tears running down his face. He reached over and hugged me so tight, I had to shift my body for comfort. The heat of his breath echoed in my ear as he continued to sob. I ran my hands up and down his back to comfort him. We just held each other, and as he cried, my own tears reappeared. As much as I wanted Kevin in my life forever, I needed to be in his life in every way, which included his daughter. Knowing what I had just discovered, I didn't know if he would have the strength to grant me that. By doing so, he would have to stand up to his past and change things he may not be willing to change. That was scary, but I could not sacrifice denying myself a relationship with the most important person in his life, because of baby momma drama. I wanted it all.

He slowly pulled back to look at me. Once our eyes met and he noticed the pain and tears in my eyes he pulled me back into him.

"The last thing I ever want to do is bring you pain, Natalie." Pulling back and looking at me again. "Do you have any idea how much I love you. Do you?"

Unable to speak, I shook my head.

"You are my world. I know this is not the perfect situation, but believe me I will make it better. I will sit down with Shelby tomorrow and let her know how I feel about everything and if she's not willing to accommodate me, then I will take her to court and try to get joint custody. Do you hear me?"

"Yes."

"Don't give up on us now," he said hugging me again, so tight as if to demonstrate how much he needed me. Whispering in my ear, he said "I need you, I love you, I want to marry you; I want you to have my son."

He gently kissed my lips and held me in his arms all night long. I didn't think about Shelby, Skyler, his trip to Indianapolis without me or the big blow up we just had earlier. I only thought of the last words he whispered in my ear. He loved me, wanted to marry me, and wanted me to bear his son. Hearing him say that brought several

127

questions to mind. Was he serious? Had he really gotten to the point where he saw me as his wife and the woman with whom he could raise a family? A few months had past since my abortion, but had his feelings grown to the point he could honestly have those feelings. I wanted it to be true. At that moment, my heart told me it was.

Chapter Twenty-Three

The radio alarm woke us both at 6:00 AM. I opened my eyes and saw Kevin's muscular arm reach over to press the snooze button. He pulled me close to him into a nice spoon position. I felt so secure in his arms and I knew in my heart that everything was going to work out okay. A few minutes later, we got up and showered together, washing each other's bodies and listening to Maxwell. It was a bittersweet morning that had to eventually come to an end with me dropping him off at LaGuardia Airport.

With my gift for Skyler in his hand, he kissed me and walked down the terminal to the plane to take him to the other life that was still so foreign to me. I had confidence that he was going to attempt to get things squared away with Shelby, although I didn't know how receptive she would be.

When I returned to the office, I called my parents. They seemed to be in an unusually happy mood. My mother had taken time off from her job to spend some time with my dad. He had gotten his strength back and was doing well. My mother ended the call saying they were heading out the door to see Eddie Murphy's *Nutty Professor*. I couldn't help but to smile at that.

That night I treated myself to a nice long bubble bath. I was dying to sample some of the bath beads and oils Kevin had purchased for me. Sitting there, I tried to focus on relaxing, but my mind could not help, but to focus on what Kevin was doing. Had he talked with Shelby about her controlling ways? Was she making advances towards him? Did she have a family dinner prepared when he arrived?

I glanced at my watch beside the tub and noticed it was almost 9:00. Kevin said he would definitely call, but he hadn't. I didn't want to call him, as if to check on him. I wanted to take him at his word and give him time. I needed to learn to trust him, although I didn't trust her.

129

By 10:30, my anger and curiosity got the best of me and I decided to call. I dialed the number to his cell phone. I figured by now he should be in his hotel room and could speak freely about the events of his day. After four rings, his voice mail picked up.

"Kevin, this is Natalie. I'm about to turn in, but please give me a call when you get this message to let me know you're okay." What I really wanted to ask was — why haven't you called me? Why aren't you answering your phone? What's going on? Have you spoken to Shelby about the changes that need to be made about Skyler? But, I played it cool. I needed to speak to him and I didn't want to piss him off with my questioning.

After waiting a few more minutes, I checked my cell phone voice mail to make sure I hadn't missed Kevin's call. No new messages. Okay, I'm calling. I had given him twenty minutes from the time I left the message and I could no longer sit and wonder about the "what ifs."

I dialed the number. After two rings, I heard a female voice answer. "Hello?"

Startled, my first reaction was to hang up, but hoping I had dialed the wrong number I said, "Yes, I'm trying to get in contact with Kevin Lewis." My heart was beating a mile a minute.

"May I ask who is speaking?" The sultry voice asked.

"This is Natalie." Before I could ask her who she was, she started talking.

"Well, Natalie. Kevin is in the shower right now, where I am about to join him, but I will give him your message, okay?" Click. She hung up on me.

I couldn't believe it. I put my hands over my face and screamed. I knew they were still involved.

"Lord, Lord, help me, Jesus," I cried out. My spirit had been telling me this was true, but I refused to believe it. He's been lying to me. He doesn't love me, he doesn't want to marry me, and he's just been using me. That was a hard pill to swallow because all of his words and actions proved otherwise. Of all people, I felt safe with him because he was a pastor.

I didn't know what to do, but I had to get out of my apartment. I grabbed my cell phone and purse and with my nightgown and scarf on, I headed towards my car to drive to an unknown destination. In the parking lot, I noticed a few neighbors, but didn't look their way. I was too hurt to care how I looked and too angry to do anything about it. My hands shook as I struggled to unlock the door to my car. After minutes of struggling, I finally noticed I was trying to unlock it with my office key.

Once in my car, I banged my hands on the steering wheel, crying and broken hearted. Why, Lord? Why?

Chapter Twenty-Four

The next few days were spent with me trying to consume myself in my work, venting to Janet, and avoiding Kevin's numerous phone calls. There was absolutely nothing he could say to me at this point.

He didn't bother to call me back that night, but all of a sudden when he's free from the watchful eye of Shelby, he's trying like hell to make contact.

By Tuesday morning, I had three days of no contact with him, but he was still calling every thirty minutes until one o'clock in the morning. It was hard, but I had to make every attempt not to contact him, because once I would he had a way of smooth talking his way back into my life. I had to continuously remind myself that he was a wolf in sheep's clothing. If there was ever a sign of me weakening, Janet would be there to remind me he was a dog and bring me back to reality.

On a business side, I had not been so motivated in a long time. I spent my work day running my morning meetings, taking out a new or weaker sales person in the field to show them the ropes, returning to the office midday to return business calls, conduct my interviews, do paperwork, welcome my salespeople back from the field, and hold training sessions for those who needed it at the end of the day. I was determined to have my business be the best it could be, despite my failing love life.

Returning home, I checked my voice mail and realized I had four messages, one from my dad and three from Kevin. I didn't even bother listening to Kevin's messages, instead opting to save them once I heard his voice. I sat on my couch and called my dad.

"Hey, Natalie. What's going on?" His voice was upbeat.

"Not much. How are you doing?"

"I'm feeling fine." He then told me about all the programs he watched on TV that day. His life had slowed down drastically due to his heart, but he always remained chipper. "You still coming down on Saturday, aren't you?"

I had totally forgotten I had booked a flight to Dallas that weekend. With all that I had going on, it had slipped my mind. I needed to get away and was now energized with the reminder of the upcoming trip. "Yeah, I'll definitely be there. Have you been feeling okay?"

"Well, I guess as well as to be expected. I just don't have any energy."

"Have you been taking your medicine? What are the doctors saying?"

"I don't think those doctors really even know what all's wrong with me. I think they are just trying to keep me comfortable. I'm not in any pain, so I guess that's a blessing." He let out a little chuckle.

"That's good. Where's Momma?"

"She's out in the back yard watering the grass." He paused. "I was just calling to let you know that if anything were to happen to me, I want you to have the Taurus," he said somberly.

My heart pounded. "What do you mean if anything happened to you, I thought you said you were feeling fine?"

"I am, but Natalie, I just don't see myself getting any better," he said in a very honest voice. "I'm gonna tell your momma about you getting the Taurus, so she knows that's what I want."

I was speechless and caught off guard. How do I respond to that? "Okay, but you are feeling fine, right?" I asked, needing that reassurance.

"Yeah, I feel fine. Hold on, while I got you on the phone, let me write down your flight information." There was a few seconds pause and he returned and wrote down the flight info. Then added, "I'll let you go, so I can go call your momma in here before those mosquitoes eat her alive. You are my heart, Natalie. I just want you to know that, you hear?"

My voice was shaky when I said, "Yes, I know. I love you and I'll see you Saturday."

"I love you, too."

After I hung up the phone, I immediately started to cry. Even though his voice sounded upbeat, he was talking like he was going to die. Was he giving up hope of getting better? Why did he feel it necessary to let me know what he wanted me to have? Was my family withholding information about his condition? I picked up the phone and called my sister. She talks to my mother every day and if there's anything going on, she would know.

"Hello."

"Hey, Veronica."

"Hi, what's up?"

"Have you spoken to Daddy lately?" I asked.

"Yeah, I spoke to him earlier today. Why, what's up?"

"Did he sound funny? I mean was he talking any differently."

"Like how?"

I repeated almost verbatim the conversation I had with him just moments ago. She grew quiet.

"No, when I last spoke to him he was just talking about how Momma had made some good fried chicken, greens and hot water cornbread for dinner. He sounded fine to me."

"So you are not aware of anything new going on with his condition?"

"No, he just told me he's been tired, but that's it." She paused then added, "I mean you know he's lost a lot of weight, but you saw that yourself when you were down last. That doesn't sound good, if he's talking like that. I don't know what to make of it."

"Do me a favor and call Momma and tell her about what he just told me and try to find out if she's heard him say anything like that."

"I most certainly will," she responded definitively. "If she tells me anything weird, I'll let you know."

"Please do. Regardless, I'll be down on Saturday. Until then keep your ears open and keep me updated."

Chapter Twenty-Five

I had a lot of time to reflect on my life on the three-hour plane ride to Dallas. Looking out the window over the massive billowy clouds, I was reminded how precious life was. I thought about my dad, about Kevin and my life without both. I had never felt so unsure about so many things. What I was sure about was even though Kevin was no longer in my life, there was no way I could even imagine my life without my dad. I had to see him.

The pilot made the announcement that we were now making our final descent into the Dallas area and I smiled with relief. Exiting the airplane, I looked through the many faces to see a familiar one. After I waited a few minutes, I walked to the baggage claim area to see if my parents were there. No one was to be seen. Stepping outside, I eventually saw the infamous green Taurus and hurried towards it. My dad was driving!! This was good to see because my mother commented my dad's fatigue and dizzy spells kept him from driving. Seeing this as a sign things were looking up, I ran towards the car with high hopes and eager anticipation.

Once I got into the car, my mother attacked me with questions like what took me so long and didn't I know to come outside to find the car, instead of making them wait. I tried to defend myself telling her I thought they would be waiting in the terminal, but I gave up, not wanting to fuel the argument anymore. I tried not to think negatively about my mother's fussing, realizing she was probably stressed with taking care of my dad and the airport traffic, but I could not help but to feel angry because the energy in the car was now cold and tense, instead of welcoming and joyous.

I sat in the back seat, mad. No one was talking. My dad had not even said anything, but a quick hello. When my mother was mad she had a way of changing the atmosphere from hot to cold. From the backseat, I looked at my dad's reflection in the rear view mirror. Although I could tell he had lost more weight, his face was still handsome and for the first time I looked at his eyes, noticing my eyes were like his, not only the shape, but also the tension inside them.

136

Midway home, he pulled the car over on the side of the highway and said I should probably drive the rest of the way. As we opened our car doors and stepped out to switch seats, I finally got the hug I was anticipating when I first approached the car. I was not fazed by the many cars whizzing by, only caring that I was in my daddy's arms, arms that had obviously deteriorated to the size of my own.

After we made it home, we relaxed on the bed he had recently made his own. He had so many medical devices, that it was just easier and more convenient for him to sleep in the room that was once mine. He disclosed the fact that he wanted to check into getting a heart transplant, but because of his age of sixty-two, it would be unlikely he would be eligible for one. He mentioned that he still had a lot of life in him and that he wanted to live, so he was thinking about going to Parkland, instead of the VA to explore other medical options. After a while, I remembered I brought the movie *Soul Food* for him to watch. On my visits, I always tried to bring a movie for him to see at home, since attending the movie theater was becoming more and more difficult for him to do. We went into the living room to start the movie and my mom joined us later.

The movie was good and they both seemed to enjoy it. I heard my dad ask for his medicine and my mother got up and shortly returned with his medication and a glass of water. As soon as Terry discovered Miles having sex on the roof, I heard my mother scream. "Natalie, there's something wrong with Edward." I looked over and saw that my dad's head had fallen straight back and I ran over to see that his mouth was wide open and his eyes had rolled back inside his head, showing only the whites.

"Run, go get help!" I yelled and quickly saw my mom burst out the door.

I ran to the hall to get the cordless phone and called 911. Hysterically, I returned and straddled my dad, begging and pleading for him to stay with me. Tears flooded down my face as I cried out louder and louder, "Don't leave me! Don't you dare leave me! Daddy, don't go!"

I gently slapped his face, which was losing signs of life every second, to try to bring him back. My mother burst through the door with a neighbor, where they laid him on the floor and administered CPR. I stood back, helpless, not knowing what to do. I then heard the ambulance's sirens approaching, so I ran out of the house and stood in the street to flag down the approaching vehicle.

Once inside, everyone cleared away to allow space for the paramedics to swiftly connect several pads to his chest that attempted to shock his heart. They repeated this a couple of times, then put his lifeless body on a nearby stretcher, where his frail arm fell off the side as they carried him away.

My mother and I hurried to the car and noticed all the neighbors standing outside to witness what could be my father's final moments. We followed the ambulance to Baylor Hospital where the chaplain and someone who appeared to be a social worker or counselor met us at the entrance.

"Are you the Thomases?" the clergyman asked calmly.

"Yes, we are. Is he okay?" my mother asked hysterically.

"We are not sure. Come this way, please." We were escorted past all the waiting patients in the emergency waiting room into another room, which also appeared to be a waiting room, but no one else was there. They stayed with us while we waited for word from the doctor on what was going on. I sat on the couch and looked straight ahead, dazed, at the wall. My mother paced and used her cell phone to call Veronica to tell her what had happened. I heard her instruct her to sit tight, until we spoke to the doctor.

What seemed to be an hour later, a middle aged man, introducing himself as Dr. Petersen, walked toward me and my mother and took a deep breath. "Mrs. Thomas, I'm so sorry, but your husband didn't make it." My mother suddenly gripped my arm tightly and I immediately felt the presence of the counselor's arm around my waist, as if to catch me if I fainted. "There was nothing we could do. I'm so very sorry."

"I want to see him," I burst out. "I want to see him, can I please see my daddy, Doctor? Please," I begged, needing to see him one more time.

"Sure, just give us a minute and we will come get you, okay. Again, I'm very sorry." I walked over to my purse and grabbed the cell phone to call Kevin. The phone rang twice and he picked up. Before he could say anything, I told him I just lost my dad and the emotion of saying those words made me lose it. I felt light-headed and the support of the counselor led me to a nearby seat. My mother grabbed the phone and I vaguely heard her say something like we'll see you when you get here. My mother joined me on the couch where she took the place of the counselor and held me, rocking me like I was a little girl, as if to soothe my pain. Pain I'm sure she was feeling, too.

Then she said something I had not realized, but was probably true, "He waited for you, Natalie. He waited for you."

The doctor led us into a room where my dad was lying. He was stretched out on a table and covered with a white sheet, leaving only his bare shoulders and face exposed. I just stood there trying to engrave every line, feature, and shape of his face in my memory. There was still a tube in his mouth, from where I assume they were trying to revive him. My mother's arm was around me. I wasn't sure if it was there to give me support, or because she needed it. After a few minutes of staring at his lifeless body, I lowered my head and kissed him on his cheek, which was still warm. We then turned and walked out of the room, looking back at his body on the table knowing life would never be the same.

* * *

Kevin's assistance was so helpful during his stay. With all of our minds on our loss, he was the rock that kept everything steady. He helped us with the heart-wrenching responsibility of calling loved ones and arranging the services for the funeral.

When it was time for the family to view my dad's body for the first time, before the wake, I felt my knees buckle. I grabbed Kevin closer for support. A cold sweat broke out all over my body and a wail sat on my chest that I did not release. My dad did not look the same. His face was puffy and at least four shades darker. Kevin consoled me as I looked at the man that I found hard to recognize as my own dad.

After the funeral, Kevin kept a close eye on me. He tended to my family's every need. Whether it was running to the store, welcoming guests into the home, or being a shoulder for me and my mother to cry on, he was there. He read Bible scriptures and prayed with us daily. I don't know what I would have done if he hadn't come.

On Sunday, he called his church to get an update on how services were. By the smile on his face, I assumed things went well in his absence. I heard him ask about how much money they brought in and then he responded, "Okay, that's about like it was last week, huh?"

Later that afternoon he tried to explain the events of the night when Shelby answered his cell phone. He said that, "Chances are I was giving Skyler her bath when you called. That's Shelby's way of trying to manipulate my happiness. She knows I've moved on and now she's trying to sabotage it. She never told me that you called and looking back, I know she erased your number from the incoming call feature on my phone and deleted any voice mail you may have left. She's silly that way." He paused and turned to look directly at me and added " I don't want Shelby. I want you. I dropped everything to be with you and I wouldn't have it any other way. She is my past; you are where my heart is. You are my future."

"I have to leave tomorrow. I have a meeting with the builders about the house. You know they told me they can have it finished in a couple of months?"

"Really, that's great Kevin," I said trying to sound excited for him. Kevin was building this quarter of a million dollar home that I wasn't sure I would be living in. Truth be told, it brought out even more insecurities in me because that was just one more thing that he possessed that could draw women to pursue him even more.

140

"Everything is gonna be all right, Natalie. I will make sure you will always be okay." I took him at his word. I needed to believe him. I had just buried the most important person in my life. I wasn't about to lose Kevin, too.

Chapter Twenty-Six

Fall was definitely here. It was evident in the changing of the colors of the leaves and the briskness of the air. Kevin had invited me to Chicago and made plans for us to spend a few days at a bed and breakfast in Wisconsin during my stay.

He realized I was still mourning my daddy's death and figured the visit would be good for me. I felt our relationship, with the exception of issues regarding Skyler and Shelby, had strengthened. He had been there for my family and me during our most difficult challenge and was constantly confessing his feelings for me. I knew our love could overcome most obstacles and I felt he knew that, too. My heart told me he was going to propose to me during my visit. Since my father's death, the idea of the institution of marriage and family relationships were even more important to me, not to mention not wasting time. We had known each other for almost two years now and had already tackled several obstacles. Whenever I mentioned marriage he did not shy away from topic, yet he rarely brought it up on his own. He knew it was important to me and he said spending the rest of his life with me was important to him. I needed to know that I was someone he could consider marrying and if I wasn't, we were simply wasting each other's time.

Sunday morning Kevin woke up before me and I could hear him praying in the other room. I couldn't make out what he was saying, but I assumed he was in prayer for the church service. I lay in his bed feeling good that I was in his world for a change. There were boxes everywhere in preparation for his move to his new home. It was a home I hoped to share with him to raise our family.

Kevin was very proud, almost to the point of arrogance, about the purchase of his house. He would often say, "Three years ago I would not have thought I would ever be moving into a home worth over a quarter of a million dollars, have a top of the line Lexus, and be able to fly first class wherever I go." I hadn't heard him give thanks to God yet.

Kevin had showered, dressed and was practically out the door before I got out of the bed. He said he would return around ten to pick me up and for me to please be ready. After a quick kiss goodbye, he was out the door. I walked into the restroom to turn on the shower and I realized I hadn't heard the phone ring since I arrived the night before. Waiting for the hot water, I walked to the phone and noticed the ringer was off. I quickly went downstairs to find that phone's ringer was off, too. The Caller ID light was blinking and I observed the digital sixteen missed calls. Something was not right. I reflected back to a conversation where Kevin said the church always calls his cell phone if they need him because while at home he needed peace and quiet. Then who was calling him? I chose not to spy, figuring with observation he could easily notice I reviewed the calls.

After my shower, I put on my new black dress I had bought a few days before, knowing I had to be stunning. I wanted Kevin to be able to look at me from the pulpit and see the First Lady of his church in me, even if I didn't see it in myself... yet.

I was astounded at how much the church had grown. The membership had exploded from about fifty to over five hundred, not including the women's choir. I sat on the sixth row from the front. It allowed me to see everyone. There were the typical three to four tardy women dressed in outfits more appropriate for after five wear than for church. They made their grand entrance, swishing in after everyone else was there to model their most recent purchases from the mall. All of them sat on either the second or third row and crossed their curvaceous legs. Sister Lula Mae Moon was still there. I spotted her sizing the women up, looking at them from head to toe as they strutted towards their seats. She then leaned over to her long-time church buddy, Sister Walker, and whispered in her ear something about the women who just strolled in. She didn't try to hide the fact that she was talking about the women. She didn't care.

As the oldest member of the church, she still ran the show. I couldn't help but smile, after seeing her lead devotion, go in the choir to lead a song and then slowly make her way back down in front of the church to do the announcements. She still had a lot of energy to be over eighty years old. And she showed no signs of slowing down. I'm sure if she did, she would die. Kevin had mentioned that other members wanted to be more involved with certain roles and assume certain positions that Sister Moon had, but she wasn't having it. She was quick to remind everyone that her daddy was one of the three founding members of this church. The church was her whole life and no one was going to take her place as long as she had her say.

I reached for my purse and pulled out a couple of dollars for the benevolent offering. I then remembered that Kevin told me he suspected the deacons of stealing the cash, so I put the money back in my purse and pulled out a handful of change instead. A few minutes later, I observed Deacon Richards and Edwards collect the baskets of money from the ushers and head towards the back to collect their undocumented pay.

It's amazing how being involved with the preacher made you privy to a lot of mess going on in the church. I would have never known that the church was a reflection of life. It had its share of theft, ego-tripping, lust, adultery, homosexuality and fornication.

After the choir sang a moving rendition of "Ain't No Way's Tired," one of the tardy church models with the tight dress and big legs rose from her second row seat and twisted to the front of the church. She was definitely strutting, waving to some and winking to others as she stood at the podium. In the most sultry voice allowed in a place of worship, she seductively started by saying, "Giving all praises to God and to our wonderful Pastor Lewis," she paused and smiled at him, "would all of our visitors please stand and give your name and church home."

It was like deja vu. I flashed back over two years when I was faced with the nervousness of what to say, but now it was different. I was practically the pastor's fiancé and the confidence that came with that fact gave me the words. "Good morning. Giving all praises to my Lord and Savior Jesus Christ. I remember many of you. My name is Natalie Thomas and I was a member here a couple of years ago before moving to New York. It is definitely wonderful being in the house of the Lord." I then took my seat. I purposely did not mention the pastor, figuring if he wanted the church to know about us, he would do it. I was eager to hear if he would give me recognition of any kind once he gave his pastoral remarks. Until then, I listened to a young man a few rows behind me give his name and church home.

"We would love to thank you for visiting with us and please come again." The attractive brick house smiled, revealing a small gap in her teeth behind her bright red lipstick, and she walked her small runway back to her seat.

There was something unsettling about her. There were always a small percentage of women in any given church that had eyes for the pastor and my money was on her being one of them. I needed to watch out for that one.

Kevin approached the pulpit podium looking extremely handsome, wearing a huge smile and his favorite blue suit. I could see why it was his favorite. Kevin had mentioned that with this suit costing over $800, it flows and feels better than all of his $500 suits. By watching him up there, I was reminded of the stunning presence he had. I was positive that some of these heifers wanted him, but I trusted him. He loved me.

The few women that pranced in late were attractive, but in a cheap and trashy kind of way. They definitely didn't fit what I felt he would be attracted to.

"Thank you, Sister Lula Mae Moon, for leading a very moving devotion," he paused and made eye contact with her and added, "That took me back. Sounded like that old time religion, didn't it, church?" There were some amens. "Nobody can pray like Sister Lula Mae Moon. There's wisdom in her praise. You take us back and we love you for it."

Sister Moon was grinning from ear to ear. She loved attention of any kind and she was eating it up. Kevin had mentioned that he singles her out to keep her happy because when she's not periodically acknowledged, she can stir up more mess than a woman sixty years younger. Plus, she tithes heavily and whenever she's pissed off for whatever reason she ends up on the sick and shut-in list needing prayer for a sore hip or arthritis, keeping her tithe money locked securely in her trademark black patent leather purse.

"The choir is singing like they are ready to record a CD. God bless you. To all of our visitors, welcome. I want to say a special hello to Sister Thomas. It is great seeing you again. Sister Thomas was a member a couple of years ago when the church was going through its building phase and she was a faithful member and active worker in our church. It's good to have you visit with us again."

I returned the acknowledgment with an artificial smile. I felt slighted, but I knew he had to conceal our involvement. As a preacher, I assumed he wouldn't say, "Hey, church, this is my girlfriend, the woman I will marry and the lady I've been fornicating with for over a year." The repercussion of disclosing any of it would be too much to bear, especially since he had not even popped the question yet. But, I was determined not to let his lack of romantic recognition ruin my joyous spirit of the day. At least he recognized me. The fact of the matter was that it didn't matter if everyone else knew; we knew the significance we had in each other's lives. Although I couldn't help but wish he had said something to insinuate my connection to be something other than a former member, if for no other reason than to let the church hussies know the real deal.

After church, I was greeted by several members and was pleased when my old friend, Soror Hazel Walker walked up to me and embraced me as if saying, "I missed you." She still looked good. Her long, salt and pepper hair was perfectly styled and she was wearing a white suit with pearls around the collar. She was in a hurry because her husband was ill and she had to go home to check on him and make his dinner. She said she would be giving me a call real soon to catch up on things.

After she left, I stood around, not knowing exactly what to do. Most members were in line to shake the pastor's hand and I decided to do the same. When I approached him, I was given a generic greeting. I walked outside the church to where several members had gathered to converse and say their goodbyes. I could feel eyes on me and I looked around to see two of the big-legged church amazons standing a few feet behind me, talking about something that seemed juicy. I noticed how each would sneak looks at me from time to time, trying not to make it obvious. When I caught the one who acknowledged the visitors look at me, she smiled. I smiled back, which I assumed gave her the courage to walk over to me.

"Hello, Sister Thomas?" She asked as if she wasn't quite sure she remembered my name. She had a slight southern accent, like she could have been from Alabama or Mississippi.

"Yes, hello. How are you doing?" I responded.

"I'm blessed. I'm sorry I was staring, but I was just admiring your outfit."

"Thank you so much, I appreciate it. Your dress is out of sight, as well," I lied.

The Amazon smiled and said, "Thank you. Where are you from again?"

"I live in New York."

"Really, I have family up there. Where about in New York?" All of a sudden I felt very uncomfortable because she was obviously probing.

"Not far from Manhattan, have you heard of Ronkonkoma?"

"Ronkonkoma," she repeated. "No, I haven't. What brings you back to Chicago?"

I was tempted to avoid this question. There was no doubt in my mind that this lady was trying to get info. I figured she was trying to pursue the pastor and was sizing up possible competition.

Just then, I heard a honk and noticed the Amazon's friend in the driver's seat of a Lexus Sports Coupe. "Is that your friend?" I asked, trying to get the attention off the question she had just asked.

She paused and looked as though she was trying to decide whether to wait for the answer to the question she had just asked or to hurry to catch her ride. Not to take the chance of sounding too nosy, she ended by saying, "Yeah, that's my girl. It was nice meeting you, Sister Thomas. Natalie, right?"

"Yes, same here. What's your name again?" I asked, realizing I hadn't gotten it.

"Oh, yeah, I'm sorry. I'm Evelyn Diggs. Take care, now." She said as she twisted towards the Lexus and glided in the passenger's seat.

Something was definitely up with her, but I was not going to give Kevin the third degree over Sister Diggs. I would just keep that name in my memory and see if it ever presented itself again. I turned over the church program and wrote the name down, deciding not to trust my memory. It could be as innocent as her having a crush on Kevin, but I knew with the assertiveness of her questioning that it could be more.

I walked up the stairs to the pastor's office where I saw a new set of people counting the money from what I remembered. Both middle-aged women looked from their counting duties and noticed me as I knocked on the door.

"Come in." I opened the door and saw Kevin seated at his desk looking over what appeared to be his phone messages.

"I didn't know where to meet you," I said as I walked in, feeling a little lost.

"No, you're okay. Have a seat. I'm just finishing up." We sat in silence for a few minutes when a knock on the door broke his concentration. "Yes," he responded. One of the new counters walked in and gave him what appeared to be the financial logbook.

"Pastor," she stopped talking when she saw me, "is this a good time for me to review the totals with you?"

"Sure, go right ahead. You remember Sister Thomas, don't you?" he said. "Sister Randal, this is Sister Thomas."

"Hi," she said as she extended her hand to shake mine.

"Okay, the total came to $19,152.25. That breaks down to $14,452 in tithes and $4,700.25 in offerings," she reported as she removed her glasses.

"Good, thank you Sister Randal. I appreciate your staying to help out."

"Not a problem, Pastor, anytime. If there's nothing else, I'm gonna go on home now."

"Please, go on. Thanks again." After the door closed, he smiled and then looked at me and said, "Remember when you were attending here we were doing only about $3,000 a Sunday? God is good. He's also right on time because I can use a lot of this money to close on the house." He started to chuckle.

"So you can do that?" I asked, adding, "take as much money from the tithes and offerings as you like?" I had to catch myself because I could only imagine what my facial expression looked like. Was this embezzlement? I assumed there had to be a process or at least a protocol to use money other than his salary. Could he just take it?

"Of course I can. Now, I don't abuse the fact that I can, nor do I make it a practice to take money from the church, but from time to time, yeah, I mean, it's really no different than you and your business." He paused, "Shoot, I've known my deacons to have had their hands in the cookie jar on more than one occasion, which is a definite no-no. But as the pastor, sure you can bonus yourself. That's all it is." I guess he noticed the disbelief in my eyes and said, "Natalie, don't look at me like that. You bonus yourself money, right?" he added in a matter-of-fact tone, knowing the answer to the question before he even asked it.

"You know I do. Especially when my dad was ill and I made all those trips to Dallas every weekend."

"Well, did you have to answer to anyone? Did anyone question how you were going to use the money?"

"No, and it was no one's business. I have sole authority over my business account and the only other signer on the account is my accountant and she cannot write any checks without my authorization." I paused, "I don't abuse it, I never have and I've always paid myself enough through my salary where I never have to touch it. The financial strength of my company has always been very important and I've never used the cash flow my guys generate for anything, but business," I then added and smiled, "...with only a few exceptions, I guess."

Kevin walked around his desk and leaned against the front of it and added, "Same here. Look," he took a deep breath as if he was searching for the right words not to give me the wrong impression, "I don't have a board of directors or any elders of the church dictating what I do or don't do like many of these other churches. I formed the church bylaws to assure that. Preachers are very similar to CEOs. I make the final call on 95% of what goes on here. It's a lot of pressure." He chuckled. "Whoever said ministry is like a business, could not have made it plainer."

That night Kevin and I went for a drive to Chicago's south side for some rib tips. It was a beautiful night. The stars were out and the temperature was just right. Kevin had the windows rolled down and the sunroof back. As I sat in the passenger seat of his new Lexus LS 430, I realized how this car was so much like him. The alluring new car scent, the sleek black leather interior with golden brown maple accent trim, the numerous lights highlighting the features on the dashboard and the voice activated navigation embodied all the class and style he possessed.

Our conversation was light, but liquid; we laughed, joked and made small talk like we'd been together for years. We talked about the service and different members old and new. I purposely did not bring up the women I had noticed at the church. The time was not right. I was having too much fun to rock the boat or show signs of what he might detect as insecurity.

150

He pulled into *Herman's Ribs and More* and an attractive black man in his early fifties who was accompanied by an equally attractive, much younger woman, met us in the parking lot. They were dressed as if they had attended church earlier that day.

"Hey, Rev. What's been up?" the man said as he embraced Kevin.

"Jackson, my man. What's been going on?"

"Not much. Hey, this is Stephanie." He motioned towards the young lady at his side. "Stephanie, this is Reverend Lewis. We go way back." He burst out into a hysterical laugh and slapped Kevin on the arm. He then made eye contact with me.

"Jackson, this is Natalie," Kevin said realizing he had not introduced me. This apparently was an old friend that had a lot of history with Kevin, judging from the laughter and slap of the arm.

I smiled, said my hello and shook the hands of both. It was interesting listening to Kevin speak to Jackson. His speech, which was normally proper, was gone. The articulation of each word was nowhere to be heard. I was witnessing a jive talking Kevin. It made me giggle. It was so weird hearing this side of him.

"Man, how you been? You looking sharp as ever, you still the pastor of that church? How's that going?" he asked. I was amazed how he jammed so many questions in two seconds.

"Man, Jackson, thing's are good. You need to come and visit one Sunday. I have about seven hundred members now between two services." Kevin said, obviously elevating his numbers to impress Jackson.

"That's good, man. I'm gonna have to visit you. I can't make any promises; you know Rev. Douglass keeps me pretty busy. You know we are up to five thousand. Man, God is good."

"You got that right. Listen, man I'm not going to keep you. But, it sure was good seeing you again. Gimme me a call sometime." Kevin said.

"I will. I most definitely will. You still at the same place "

"Yeah, well for now. You know I'm building a home in Arlington Heights."

"Big timer. Man, you on the ball!"

Three loud laughs, about four or five "mans," and an embrace later Jackson and his date said their goodbyes and walked towards their car.

Standing in the long line waiting to place our to go order, Kevin told me that Jackson was Shelby's cousin. Once Shelby and Kevin's relationship ended, they lost contact. He went on to say that Jackson was an usher at one of the biggest churches in Chicago and was a womanizer. He had at least six children, three from three different women at his own church and rumored to have one from a woman at Kevin's. He went on to add that Jackson wanted a church at one time, but shied away from the idea knowing his history for his weakness for women would hinder his dream.

"Are he and Shelby close?" I asked, hoping they were and Jackson would communicate to Shelby about the encounter with Kevin and me.

"They're okay, I guess. I really don't know. My contact with Shelby is limited and I haven't seen Jackson in over three years. So, I wouldn't know. Why?"

"Just asking," I responded, keeping my response short and simple, not wanting to press for information.

Chapter Twenty-Seven

It was only a little over a two hour drive to the bed and breakfast in Wisconsin. The trip down was breathtaking, magnified by the mixture of the different colors along the highway, the jazz sounds of Boney James newest CD, and the sporadic words of endearment Kevin would say. He was definitely in a romantic mood. When Kevin reached over and caressed my hand, I knew in my gut he would ask me to marry him. All the signs were there. We had promised to be focused on one another, which meant no cell phone or other distractions.

We turned into the small graveled driveway, which led to a magnificent, two-story, white Victorian home. On the massive porch sat two rocking chairs that looked very welcoming. As we walked up the stairway and knocked on the door, we were greeted by an older white woman dressed in a white, flowing comfortable dress with flowers stitched around the collar. The outfit reminded me of the housedresses my grandmother wore around the house.

"Well, good morning. You must be the Lewises," she said in a sweet, meek and frail voice.

I looked up and smiled at Kevin, liking the sound of what I had just heard. I assumed he just made the reservations under his name and the old woman just assumed I was his wife, which was fine by me.

"Yes, pleased to meet you." Kevin extended his hand.

"Well, just call me Mama Louise. Come on in. You are right on time for some breakfast. But, first, let me show you to your room."

As we walked in, I noticed the shine of the hardwood floors and the understated, yet comfortable furniture. The Victorian home was very well taken care of and smelled of what I could detect to be sausage and eggs.

The atmosphere of the house made me feel good all over. It felt like grandma's house. The furniture could be dated back to the sixties, but was in excellent condition. All the wooden furniture looked freshly polished with a nice shine. On almost every table there were family photos, which could have represented every generation from the twenties to current.

Kevin picked up our single bag and followed Mama Louise and me to a beautiful room decorated with flowing chantilly lace curtains that covered a huge window overlooking a pond in the backyard. In the middle of the room sat a huge, canopied, Victorian, king-sized bed with pink floral satin sheets with matching shams, pillowcases and comforter. On the cherry wood dresser was a vase with fresh red roses.

"This is beautiful. Thank you, Mama Louise," I said.

"You're welcome, Sweetie. Your towels and toiletries are in the bathroom," she pointed to the visible doorway near the corner of the room. "If there is anything, I mean anything you need, just holler. Whenever you are ready to eat, come on downstairs. I'll keep it warm for you."

Kevin walked in and put the bag down. "Thank you. Everything is lovely, Mama Louise. We'll be down shortly."

Kevin closed the door and stepped towards me and hugged me, while whispering in my ear, "You like it?"

"Like it, I love it," I said gazing into his eyes.

After breakfast we took a nap, for what seemed to be three or four hours. I woke before Kevin and lay quietly in his arms, anxious about our romantic get away and even more anxious about what it would reveal.

The remainder of the day was filled with touring the many beautiful sites of the state. Wisconsin was filled with postcard-pretty valleys, dramatic bluffs, and crystal blue lakes. I could not have chosen a more beautiful backdrop to spend the day with Kevin. Being drawn to the scenery, Kevin pulled the car to a small park, right off the interstate. We walked leisurely along a trail that eventually opened to reveal a luscious pasture home of the largest oak trees and wildlife imaginable. We were amazed at all the squirrels, birds and deer in this one pasture. Kevin later discovered a stream that served as a source of water for the wildlife. He thought that was possibly the reason for the grass being such a rich color of green.

Arriving back at the bed and breakfast, we were exhausted. We laid down for a minute and went downstairs for dinner. I was shocked to walk into the dining room to see that Mama Louise had prepared a steak dinner by candlelight for us. I assumed Kevin had arranged it. We were her only guests, but I had a feeling she didn't do all this for every guest.

Kevin pulled out my chair and then sat across from me. "Looks like Mama Louise really went all out for us."

"Yeah, you think," I said facetiously. "This looks good. Everything does. Look at this china, Kevin."

"I see." He looked at the delicate trimming around the plate. "This place came highly recommended. I wanted you to have a nice time. We needed to have a nice time. Let us pray," He reached his hand to hold mine. "Heavenly Father, we would like to give thanks for the meal in front of us and the hands that prepared it. Lord, have this meal to nourish our minds, body and spirits. We pray this in the name of Your Son, Jesus Christ, Amen."

"Amen." I had to admit, I was impressed. By the looks of her, you wouldn't imagine she could prepare a tender, thick steak topped with sliced sautéed mushrooms and some type of sprout I couldn't identify. She also had fresh mixed vegetables with cheese sauce and a Caesar salad. The meal was picture perfect and I almost hated to disturb the masterpiece on the china. I ate carefully by taking my time and consuming small bites, trying to look as cute as possible through the candlelight. Tonight I needed him to see me as possessing the qualities he wanted in a wife and steak between my teeth or cheese sauce on my chin would easily distort that image. He looked so handsome, so masculine, so much like all I had ever wanted in a man. I needed him to want me, to need me, to desire me.

"Let's go upstairs," Kevin said as his eyes locked seductively with mine across the dinner table. He stood up and walked over to my seat and held out my chair, then grabbed my hand as we proceded upstairs to our cozy room.

My heart was beating fast. I followed him into the room, where he immediately sat me on the edge of the king-sized bed. He then reached into the overnight bag and pulled out a black piece of fabric. Walking back to me, he stopped at the nightstand and turned on the small radio, which just happened to be playing *Zoom* by the Commodores. He reached behind me and tied the fabric around my head to blindfold me.

"What are you doing?" I questioned.

"Shhh," he whispered, putting his finger over my lips.

I heard him walk out the door, down the hall, and down the stairway. What was going on? Lord, give me strength. I was so anxious I could hear my heart beating. I sat quietly for about a minute. I heard footsteps approaching and the door open. I could feel his presence in front of me, but he still had not said a word. I felt his hand on the back of my head untying the small knot. When the blindfold fell, I saw Kevin standing in front of me holding a small burgundy jewelry box.

My Lord. I couldn't breathe. This was it! He was about to ask me the question I had longed to hear since the first day I met him.

"Go ahead, open it," he said smiling the biggest smile I had ever seen him display. I reached my hands up and slowly opened the box that hid the symbolism of our future. As the box creaked open, I saw what had to be an eighth of a karat, diamond ring with a gold band. I looked up at him and smiled, not really knowing what this ring was suppose to indicate. It was clearly too small to be an engagement ring.

Confused, I had no idea how to respond. I put on my acting hat and said in my most convincing tone, "Kevin, it's beautiful." I didn't know what to think. Was this his way of asking me to marry him? There was no "Will you marry me?" or no getting down on one knee. I searched his eyes for answers, but came up empty. I then came into the realization that Kevin was in the process of moving into a quarter of a million dollar home, drove a fifty thousand dollar car and wore eight hundred dollar suits. There's no way this small, $500 ring could represent an engagement from a man that had such expensive taste, but I had to know for sure.

I looked at him, with the biggest smile I could muster and enthusiastically asked, "So, does this mean we should set a date?"

He paused and said, "I love you, Natalie. I love you more than I've loved any woman in my life. I hope you realize that," he took a deep breath, "sure, yes. I think we should look at making everything official by this time next year." In a strange way, he responded like I had asked him to marry me.

This time next year? What was the delay? We had known each other for a long time and had been dating for over a year. Was this ring a ploy to make me feel secure in our relationship or to shut me up about my value or place in his life? To pacify me by allowing him to still see me without the indirect pressures of marrying me? I looked into his eyes and decided not to let this moment be stolen with speculation. He wanted to marry me, and just because that fact was not in the dressing I had hoped for, the truth still remained, and he bought me an engagement ring. I waited for him to put the ring on my finger, but when the minutes dragged on, I took the miniature ring out of the box and put it on my finger, hoping it would look bigger on. It didn't. This was not how it was supposed to be.

He then gently grabbed my hand and held it, looking at the ring and said, "You wear it well, Natalie."

"Thank you," I responded, thinking he had to be kidding.

Chapter Twenty-Eight

"Girl, you are glowing. I take it your romantic get-away to Chicago did you some good?" Janet said as she entered my office with a cup of coffee for me.

I looked up from my mail and smiled. "I would say so," I said as I flashed the ring on my left hand.

"Oh my God!" Janet screamed and grabbed my hand. She took a long look at the ring and then added, "So, what does this mean? You guys jumping the broom?"

"What do you think?"

"I have learned not to assume anything. So, he asked you to marry him?" she blurted out enthusiastically.

I didn't know exactly how to answer. I knew that if I gave her too much information about how he never officially asked in the traditional way, she would easily burst my bubble. Instead, I gave my own answer, "Yes, we are getting married."

"Oh, my God, Natalie," she walked around my desk and hugged me in a rocking motion. "I am so happy for you."

"Thank you. "

"So how did he do it?" she pried.

I answered carefully by focusing on giving elaborate details about the ride to Wisconsin, the scenery of the lakes and pastures, the bed and breakfast and all the romantic moments that led up to his presenting me with the ring. She was so excited for me; she didn't seem to notice I left out the lack of an official proposal.

"You guys set a date? I need to know so I can start losing a few pounds. I am in your wedding, right?" she said, still beaming with joy.

"We haven't ironed out all the details, but it will probably be next year, sometime. And of course, you know you are going to make a beautiful bridesmaid."

She slapped her hands and said, "Yeah, that's what I'm talking about!" then added, "You tell your mama yet?"

"Girl, yes. She was one of the first people I called. She was so happy. Ever since she laid eyes on Kevin, she asks me about him and how we are doing every chance she gets." I added, "It's bittersweet, though. I always thought my daddy would give me away at my wedding." I dropped my head.

"I know this has to be difficult for you." She spoke a little louder, "Now, from what you told me about your dad, he loved you more than life itself, right?"

I looked up. "Yes."

"Then he would want more than anything for you to be happy. Does Kevin make you happy?"

"Yes, he does. He makes me very happy. You know he does." I was now smiling.

"You go to his church when you were there?"

"Of course. Girl, it has grown so much since I left, over five hundred were there. But, I discovered there are some hoochies there that undeniably have their eyes on Kevin, but they aren't anything to worry about."

"Why is it that in every church there are women that want to get with the pastor?" Janet said. "Don't take that fact lightly, women can be ruthless. Kevin is a very attractive man and by all accounts, single in their eyes. Just watch out."

"I know. I don't like the fact I'm so far away and can't regulate things, but that soon will change. I'm sure Kevin will be making an announcement letting them know he's engaged or he may wait for my next visit to Chicago to do it. Regardless, give it some time, they all will know soon, I'll make sure of that."

The afternoon flew by. I had so much work to catch up on. Kevin called me a few times. He told me how much he missed me and that he loved me. He mentioned he was also scheduled to close on his new home in a few days and was trying to get mentally prepared for the backlash from some members that feel preachers shouldn't be able to afford to live in a home bigger than their own.

"Are members that shallow?" I asked.

"Yes. Some are, especially the old heads. I can just hear Sister Lula Mae Moon saying, "No preacher should be living in a $250,000 house."

Trying to be as encouraging as possible I said, "Well, you may lose a few, but those that support you, your anointing and the ministry will stick by you. I wouldn't worry about it."

"Oh, I'm not. I'm just preparing myself. It's coming. I can feel it."

Chapter Twenty-Nine

Saturday mornings should not be spent like this. I couldn't believe the phone company's service was this bad. I had been on hold for almost twenty minutes. But I was determined to find out information on who had been calling my house for the past three weeks, hanging up. My caller ID would display an anonymous call, giving no name or number. I wasn't about to change my number and I couldn't block a number I didn't know. The phone would ring two times, then stop and the times I answered who ever was calling would hang up in my face, although once a female voice said, "Bitch," and slammed the phone in my face. The customer service person could not trace the calls, because the person pressed *67. The only advice she was able to give was to pay to have a block, forbidding those anonymous calls from coming through or have my number changed and make sure the new one was not listed. I had no idea who could be calling me. No one in the office had my number except Janet and Christopher. I had not given my number to anyone besides a handful of close friends and family I had known for years.

I spent the remainder of my day cleaning up. My place was a mess. I just hadn't felt up to doing any chores and now I had at least two loads of laundry, a sink full of dirty dishes, vacuuming, mopping, and dusting to do. I turned the volume up on the television to hear the news from the kitchen while I started the dishes.

I could hear the newscaster say that there were severe thunderstorms coming from the Midwest and they should hit most of the east coast by Sunday. I thought about Kevin, who I had not heard from this morning, so I dried my hands and walked to the cordless phone to give him a call. I dialed his number and got his voice mail.

"Kevin, I was just calling to say good morning and to check on you. I heard there's quite a bit of rain down your way and was calling to see how you're doing. I figured you were on your bedroom balcony looking at the rainfall. Give me a call when you get this message."

161

Kevin had been so busy with the move he wasn't calling me as much as he usually did, but he would always make a point to call me to say good morning. I guess he was busy. On my way back to the kitchen, I had an urgent need to urinate. I rushed in the bathroom and could barely get down my sweat pants in time to release. I was surprised to notice that only a small amount of urine came out. I would have thought it would have been a river, but it wasn't.

By the time the news went off, I was finished with the dishes, relieved that it didn't take long at all. As I sprayed my counters with antibacterial spray, I felt a need to go to the bathroom again. I dropped my sponge on the floor and sprinted to the restroom and released only a few drops accompanied by a slight burning sensation. What was going on? I had heard about urinary tract infections from a college roommate and after an hour and four more trips to the bathroom, I figured I must have one.

I drove to Eckerd's and looked for something that would cure this thing. I picked up a package of AZO and headed towards the counter, relieved I found something to put an end to this. As I walked out the door, the urge was there again. I turned to try and find the nearest restroom, knowing I couldn't make it home in time.

I took the small orange pill as soon as I made it home and checked my caller ID and saw that Kevin had not called. I hoped he was okay. This was not like him. I then walked into the kitchen and checked my cell phone I had left on the counter and saw that there were no missed calls. By three o'clock, Kevin finally called and told me he hadn't called because he had a wedding and two funerals to do that morning and afternoon.

When I mentioned to him that he didn't mention his busy schedule to me the night before, he just said it slipped his mind.

"Well, what are you going to do for the rest of the day?" I asked.

"I need to stop by Home Depot and pick up some border for the dining room." There was a pause. I didn't know how to respond. I hated the fact that decisions were being made about the house without me. If this was to be the home where we both would live and start our lives together as husband and wife, I should be there. "Why are you so quiet?" he asked, noticing the silence.

"I wish I were there to help out," I said, "I'm feeling a little left out because I'm not a part of the decorating process."

"I know. I wish you were here, too. But I'll make sure I'll pick something out you'll like." It's just like men to give an answer to try and settle the problem, instead of going to the root of it. I knew because of geography, I couldn't be there and that was just how it was.

"I'm going to plan a trip to Chicago in a couple of weeks, okay?" I figured that would allow enough time for this bladder infection to clear up.

There was a moment of silence and then he said, "Sure, just let me check my schedule, so I can make sure I'm in town or not too busy with meetings when you're here. I'll call you with the best time later on, okay."

"Okay, let me know. I feel like I'm missing out on stuff down there. I'll let you go. I miss you."

"I miss you, too."

I hung up the phone feeling empty. Not only was I not a part of deciding on the furniture, accessories, or any other detail regarding the house, but Kevin didn't seem to be affected by it nor was he making any strides to get me down there to include me.

The next day, I had planned on going to church, but decided against it. The frequent urination had stopped, but the burning had stayed and even intensified. I even had periods of itching. I examined my vaginal area with my bathroom mirror and noticed nothing out of the ordinary.

I spent the day in my robe, so I could get away without wearing underwear to prevent further irritation. Something was definitely wrong. If things didn't get better by tomorrow, I would go to the doctor.

The rain made it a perfect day for a nap, so I reclined on my bed and tried not to think about what could be wrong with me, why Kevin seemed to be distancing himself lately, and why I don't feel as happy as I should, being engaged to the man of my dreams.

The next morning I woke up feeling awful. I was extremely fatigued from lack of sleep due to the itching and burning all night long. I also felt feverish. Knowing there was no way I could go to the office, I called Janet and Christopher to inform them I would be in later.

I was one of the first people in the waiting room to see the doctor. Since I didn't have an appointment, I made sure to be there when it opened. It was the same receptionist from my first infamous visit and as she gave me paperwork to fill out, I wondered if she remembered me. I'm glad I came in when I did because by the time I turned my paperwork in and the nurse called me in the examination room, the waiting area was full.

After my vital signs were taken and I was weighed in, she led me to the room where I waited for the doctor. Sitting in the room, I wondered how many other young girls and women had sat in the exact same spot I was in. My thoughts were distracted when the doctor came in the room. It was the same elderly doctor that had performed my abortion a few months ago. I didn't feel as shy about speaking with him about my symptoms because I knew what I had wasn't anything to be ashamed of. I was sure all I would needed was a prescription stronger than the AZO I had been taking over the weekend.

"Okay, it sounds like a bladder or urinary tract infection, but I'm going to take some blood and a urine samples to make sure there's nothing else there. The nurse will be in shortly."

The young black nurse came in and took her samples and afterwards I sat and waited. I thought about Kevin. I wondered what he was doing and if he was thinking about me. He rarely brought up the marriage and was always occupied with a meeting, counseling session, funeral, wedding, or church service. I was elated his ministry was thriving; I just really needed to know exactly where I fit into the equation. I thought with our being engaged I would have fewer questions about my place in his life, but as it turns out, I had more than ever before.

The doctor entered the room looking at his chart. "Well, Ms. Thomas, looks like you have traces of chlamydia."

My heart dropped. "Chlamydia. Isn't that a STD?" I blurted.

"Yes, it is," he said, looking up from his chart to make eye contact with me. "All of your vitals are normal, but according to your chart, I assume you are also aware of the fact that you are pregnant."

"I'm what?"

"You are pregnant. We'll have to do an ultrasound to find out how far along you are, but yes, Ms. Thomas, you are."

I lowered my head to rest in my hands. I couldn't believe it. I just couldn't believe it. I felt faint, but through all the emotions I was experiencing, I could still hear the doctor say something like I may want to consult with my sexual partners to inform them, but he was going to write a prescription to clear it up. Not knowing anything about the disease I asked, "So this is something that can be cured?"

"Yes. I'm going to give you a prescription for medication, which is a powder substance you are to take with water. It's only one dosage, but it will clear it right up. I would refrain from having any sexual intercourse until a few days after you take the medication and until your partner is treated. Make sure you use a condom even if your partner's test comes out negative; it may not show up depending upon how long he's been exposed. You wouldn't want to re-infect yourself. Do you have any questions?"

"No, sir," I answered dryly through my hands, not wanting to look at him. This was almost too much to consume. Having one diagnosis was bad enough, but I had two of the worse I could ever imagine. Kevin had given me a venereal disease and worse of all, impregnated me once again.

Chapter Thirty

I stormed out of the doctor's office in a daze. I don't remember paying the receptionist, getting in my car, or the drive back to the office. I just remember walking into my office and bursting into tears. Janet noticed and followed, closing the door behind her.

"Natalie, Natalie, what's the matter?" she asked walking up to me and gripping both of my arms, which forced me to look at her directly woman to woman, toe to toe. Unable to conceal my tears with my hands or to walk away, I just cried uncontrollably to the point where I was weak. The only thing that kept me from falling was Janet's arms grasping mine. "My God Almighty. What happened to you?"

"I need to be alone. Just leave me alone, please," I commanded, shaking my body free from her grasp. I needed to be free to spend time by myself to figure this out.

Looking at me with the deepest concern I had ever seen in her eyes, she said, "Natalie, you are more than my boss, you are a friend. There's no way in hell I'm going to let you go through whatever this is alone. I'm not going anywhere until you open up and tell me what is wrong."

Unable to hold it in any longer, I fell in her arms where I wailed tears of sorrow. After a while, my crying lessened to the point where I could say in the most broken voice I had ever heard leave my lips, "Kevin gave me chlamydia," I paused trying to hold it together as I added, "and I'm pregnant with his child. Again."

The explosive reaction I expected her to give didn't come. Instead she just held me, not saying a word. She then guided me to the chair at my desk, where I sat and looked blankly at the wall in front of me. I was at the point where my crying didn't produce tears. I made eye contact with her as she sat across from me. She now had tears in her eyes. "Natalie, I'm so sorry."

A few minutes later, I was able to talk enough to tell her about what I thought was a bladder infection and how that led me to the clinic. I told her all the information I had about the disease and about the pregnancy.

"Are you going to keep the baby, Natalie?" she asked.

"I don't know. Hell, I can't even think straight. How can I raise a child from a man that can't even be faithful to me? A man that lies and deceives? I have no idea what to do."

"Is there anything I can do for you, anything at all?"

Trying to get my head together, I gave her my prescription, insurance information and credit card and sent her to the store to fill my prescription. First things first. I had to be rid of one issue, so I could start to focus on the next. Having the chlamydia out of my system was definitely a priority and something I could do today. Then I could focus on the pregnancy.

"Also, call Christopher on his cell phone and get him back in here to conduct today's interviews. I'm not going to be any good today, but I'll be okay until you get back." I instructed in a low monotone voice.

"Not a problem," she said as she stood up and headed towards the doorway to my office.

"Thank you, Janet. Thank you for everything." After Janet left, I just laid my head on the desk. All I wanted to do was to go home and go to sleep. My mind evaluated all of the events over the past three weeks. I now knew that the distance I was feeling from Kevin was not my imagination, but directly relating to his rendezvous with other women. All the anonymous hang-ups I had been receiving were probably from a woman who Kevin was sleeping with who had gotten my number from directory assistance or his caller ID.

His ego with having a two hundred and fifty thousand dollar house, a luxury automobile, a growing church and so many women at his disposal triggered his pulling away. I realize now that the ring was never meant to be an engagement ring, but only a ploy to satisfy my desire to marry him just enough to keep me around to screw at his disposal. That's why he didn't invest the money I know he could have in the ring. A man that cares so much about image and nice, expensive things would have chosen a ring that represented the same, not something that probably didn't even cost five hundred dollars. That's why he never officially proposed or got down on one knee. It was all an act.

I was awakened by a knock on my office door. "Come in," I shouted, startled by the heavy knock. Christopher entered my office bouncing in with his trademark upbeat walk and wearing a Kool-Aid smile.

"What up, boss?" he asked, taking a seat at my desk. "Dude, you look horrible."

Christopher's personality was so pleasant and contagious. He could usually bring a smile to my face on my worst day, but this day surpassed horrible. "Thanks, Christopher. I appreciate the compliment," I said as I blew my nose.

"You sick?"

"Yeah, I came down with something. Janet is actually on her way back with my medicine. Listen, I need you to stay in the office for the rest of the day and do the interviews while I get some rest, okay?"

"Not a problem, you go get well. Are you okay? Your eyes are blood red, dude!" he said.

"I'm okay, Christopher. I just need my medicine and to get some rest and I'll be okay."

Janet walked in the office and automatically took control, sending Christopher to her desk to answer the ringing phone. He didn't protest and left the office.

"Okay, here you go," Janet said, putting the bag with the medicine on my desk along with a plastic cup of water. I immediately opened the bag, read the directions and poured the powdered potion in the water. I stirred the mixture with my finger and drank the tasteless liquid. Afterwards, I inhaled, then exhaled and felt relieved that this problem is no more.

"Thanks so much, Janet," I said while reaching down for my purse. "I'm gonna get out of here and go home. Call me later on with the totals for the day."

There was a knock at the door, and without waiting for an answer, Christopher opened the door and peeked his head in to say, "You got Kevin on line one." My heart skipped a beat. Not ready to confront that obstacle right now I said, "Tell him I'm in a meeting and I'll call him back."

"When are you going to talk to him?" Janet asked.

"When I can find the words. Right now, I'm empty. I don't know what to say. I'm just too confused to talk right now, but believe this — I will," I said, approaching the door.

"I'll call you later," Janet said as she approached to hug me. "I will be praying for your strength through this. If you need anything, call me."

Her genuine concern warmed my heart. I knew she had a lot to say. She always did. But I think I gave her too much information for even her to digest. Instead, she did what a true friend does. She didn't judge me or let me be alone; she just listened and comforted me. That was what friendship was all about.

* * *

Tossing and turning, I just couldn't get comfortable. Finally, after finding a spot that brought me comfort enough to go to sleep, the phone rang. Damn it! I allowed the phone to ring, hoping whoever was on the other line would leave a message or just hang up, but this person was persistent. I got up, thinking it might be my mother having a bad night dealing with my father's death.

"Hello?"

"May I speak with Natalie?"

"This is Natalie. May I ask who's speaking?"

"Natalie, this is Shelby. Shelby Johnson, Kevin's girlfriend." Her voice was kind and sincere. "I hope I'm not disturbing you, but we need to talk."

My heart pounded. I didn't know what to say. The infamous Shelby had called me and told me she was Kevin's woman. Remain calm, just take her lead, I told myself.

"Yes?" I said wanting to find out the purpose of her call before questioning her or giving out info.

"Natalie, I'm not calling you to start anything with you. I know you have been seeing Kevin, but if he told you he doesn't have a girlfriend, he's lying. I have been with Kevin for almost five years now."

"Okay, this is news to me."

"So, you are telling me that Kevin has never told you about us." she said sternly.

"Other than you being his baby's mother. That's it."

"Well, baby girl, where do you think he stays when he visits? I'll tell you, he stays with me, in my bed." She paused. "Listen, I know this has to be hard for you to hear, but I thought you had the right to know."

I was past furious, but I needed info. This only confirmed that he was the snake I knew he was. Lies, all lies!!! "How did you get my number, Shelby?"

"From his cell phone. You called while he was here and I answered the call, remember?" she explained.

"So you never heard about me before the phone call? Kevin has never brought me up to you? I actually bought Skyler two outfits for Kevin to bring with him to Indiana. Did you ever get them?" I pried.

There was silence, then she said, "You know what, he has brought a couple of really cute outfits, but he said they were gifts from his sister. But to answer your question, he has never mentioned your name to me. Why would he? He's been deceiving you and truth be told, me too."

My trembling hand wiped my wet face. "But, we're engaged. I'm wearing his ring."

"Baby girl, I am, too. I've been wearing it for the past year."

"I'm going to go now," I said, not needing to hear any more.

172

Chapter Thirty-One

By Wednesday morning, all the sorrow of my situation was gone. It had been replaced with anger. Kevin had called several times, but I had chosen not to answer the calls. He had to feel my pain, he needed to feel a fraction of what I was experiencing and I was convinced I couldn't achieve that over the phone. I called my travel agent for her to book me on an afternoon flight to Chicago.

He won't be able to hide behind the phone when I tell him he infected me with chlamydia. I didn't want him to make an excuse about a meeting when I told him I was pregnant with his child. A counseling session could not come between us when I brought up the Shelby phone call. I needed to confront him and there was no other option.

I called Janet to have her inform Christopher I was still under the weather and I would not be in. When I mentioned to her my plan to go to Chicago, she cautioned me that it would not be a good idea. She advised that I had no idea what I would be walking into and someone should be with me. When she offered, I told her it was something I needed to do alone.

On the plane, I changed my plan from showing up at Bible study that night to just surprising him at home. I ordered a rum and coke on the plane to calm my nerves. Several scripts of what to say played over and over in my mind. On the one hand, I wanted to slap his face for giving me a STD. Another part of me wanted to sit down with him and calmly discuss the dilemma I was faced with and hear what he had to say for himself. Still being hurt, and foolishly in love, I had no idea how it was going to come out. Regardless, it had to.

I followed the signs for ground transportation in Chicago Midway Airport. Fortunately, there was a car available. I was worried because I forgot to tell my travel agent to reserve a car for me. I got in the beige Cavalier and exited the parking lot towards I-55. I reached in the backseat for my purse to pull out the directions to his house I had gotten off Mapquest.Com. My heart raced as I exited the freeway, knowing I was less than three miles from his house. All of a sudden fear entered my body, not knowing what I was walking into. I figured he would be home, preparing for Bible study that was scheduled to start in about two hours. I turned onto the street that led to his gated subdivision and followed a Navigator SUV through. I was immediately impressed with the exclusiveness of the neighborhood. There were no homes under four thousand square feet and there were several lots where homes were still under construction. I had never seen the house before. It was being built during my last trip to Chicago. As I turned on his street, my heart pounded harder. Midway down the street I saw the home that matched the address I once thought I would share with him. His car was not parked in front of the beautiful two story brick home, so I had no idea if he was home — alone or with someone else.

I pulled the car into the driveway. I hesitated before getting out and just sat there for a few minutes. I took a deep breath, reached for my purse and reluctantly got out of the car. I walked slowly, terrified of what the next few minutes would reveal or how I would react when I saw him. I stood at the door and slowly rang the doorbell. I could hear the strong, elegant bell tone echo through the home. I couldn't hear any signs of anyone being there. The house was silent. I rang again and then heard heavy footsteps approaching.

"Who is it?" he called out.

I swallowed. "Kevin, it's me. Natalie."

I heard him say something under his breath, but I couldn't make out what it was. He opened the door and stood in the entryway.

"Natalie. What are you doing here? Why didn't you let me know you were coming?" He asked, wearing a smile, with his eyes questioning my motives, while blocking the doorway.

"Can I come in?" I asked pointing towards the door.

"Oh, my God, yes, of course. Excuse my manners." He swung open the door, allowing me to enter.

As I stepped in, I quickly scanned the entryway that led to the living room. All hardwood floors, but he had very little furniture. It didn't appear that he had company.

"I thought you said you would be coming down in a couple of weeks," he said walking towards the living room. He was dressed in blue slacks and a light blue shirt.

"That was the plan, but I needed to see you sooner," I said as I followed him through the massive living space.

"I've been calling and calling you. Are you okay?" He asked turning to look at me, noticing my serious expression. "I was just getting ready to head to the church. I have a meeting before Bible study."

I didn't want to get into everything I had to tell him now. I needed his undivided attention and I didn't feel comfortable blurting out everything I needed to say in a few minutes.

"I'm very tired. Do you mind if I hang out here until you get back?"

He looked around the room, as if he were scanning for anything incriminating. "Of course, make yourself at home. As you can see, the place is in a shambles. I'm still trying to unpack and get things in some type of order. Let me show you around."

He led me through the house. There was a new area rug and rust colored couch in the living room. He had put up a border in the dining room and bought some new black appliances for the kitchen to match the counter tops. Three of the four bedrooms upstairs were completely empty. But I noticed he had bought new bedroom furniture for the master bedroom. The most noticeable piece of furniture was a huge bed, made for a king. It had enormous round mahogany posts that stretched up to the ceiling. The bed was so tall there were steps to use to get on it. It was covered with the most masculine bedding I had ever seen. It was all shades of black. Satin black, rustic black, blue black and sheer black were all in the fabric of the plush comforter, shams and throw pillows. I couldn't help but wonder if he had shared this bed with the other woman (or women) I now knew existed. I was silent during the tour. I had nothing to say. Chances are I wouldn't be here to share it with him, so there was no need to get excited about the possibilities or give him any input.

"If you want, you can lay down here," he pointed at the bed. "As a matter of fact, this bed is only two weeks old. I paid over eight thousand dollars for the mattress." He bragged as he hopped onto the bed, choosing not to use the steps.

I was suddenly even more disgusted with him. I was willing to bet the bed was purchased with tithe money meant for the church. "No, I would rather relax downstairs. You go ahead to church. We'll talk when you get back."

"Sure you're okay?" he asked, standing up.

I turned away and walked towards the bedroom balcony. "We have to talk, but I don't want to get into it now. You go on to church. You don't want to be late for your meeting."

Kevin looked at his watch and said, "Shit, I'm late. Make yourself at home and I'll be back right after Bible study," he said as he grabbed his tie that was lying on the headboard of the bed and walked me downstairs.

I sat on the couch and picked up a *Black Enterprise Magazine* lying on the floor. I noticed how he was scurrying around, going from room to room. I smiled, knowing exactly what he was doing — getting rid of any evidence and making sure everything was in order and out of sight.

He entered the living room and walked over to kiss my cheek. He then hugged me and said, "I'm so glad you're here." All I could think of was Y*eah, right, Motherfucker. Sure you are.* "If you need me, call me, okay?" he said as he rushed out the door.

176

I waited for the garage door to close and for his car to disappear down the street before I got to work. I wanted evidence, evidence he could not deny. I was sure that once I mentioned the STD he would deny his infidelity and accuse me of being the one straying. I sprinted around the house to find the Caller ID, which would give me the names I needed. I knew he had one from my last visit. It's amazing how when you are in love you have blind eyes to the obvious.

Looking around the kitchen, I spotted the Caller ID by his cordless phone. After looking at the side of the phone, I noticed the ringer was in the "off" position. I pressed the button to display the previous fourteen calls the Caller ID had in its memory. I saw a call from his sister, three calls from the church, one call from his baby's mama, three calls that just displayed phone numbers, but no names, and three calls from Evelyn Diggs. Two of her calls were made after eleven o'clock last night.

I've heard that name before, but from where? It came to me. I ran back in the living room and picked up my purse to pull out the notepad where I had written the name of the big legged, tight-dress-wearing hoochie that had questioned me after church that day. I knew it. I knew it. It was her.

I ran upstairs and looked through his master bathroom. Many of the other rooms were empty, but I knew if Ms. Evelyn Diggs had spent any time over here, she would have left some evidence in the bathroom. I looked through the drawers and didn't see anything significant. I didn't find any make up, loose hairs, or feminine products. Bingo! I opened the shower and found a bottle of Optimum Lavish Shampoo and Conditioner. Not far from them lay a pink razor and some Nair hair removal lotion. I picked up the three pieces of evidence and threw them on his bed.

It seemed like every piece of evidence I discovered only fueled me to find more. I was like a mad woman going from room to room, searching. The living room was clean and so were three bedrooms. I opened the closet door to the master bedroom and looked through his clothes, checking his pockets for restaurant receipts or movie ticket stubs and his shirt collars for makeup. There was nothing incriminating until I reached the very back of the row of clothes. I saw two size 14 dresses, two low-cut blouses, and a mini skirt. The style and size of the clothes had Evelyn's name all over them. I also discovered a video that had *1995* written on the label. I yanked the clothes off the hangers and threw them on the bed with the other findings. Since there was no VCR in the bedroom I held on to the tape until I found one.

As I walked out of the bedroom, I noticed a door I hadn't opened. It was the laundry room. Next to the new matching shiny black washer and dryer, I saw a laundry basket with a pile of clothes. I stood looking at the dirty clothes and made the decision to look through them. I had really sank to a low level, but I just needed to see if she had any other things here. Midway through, in plain view, was a hot pink matching set of bra and panties. Without warning, I vomited. I staggered up and tried to get my balance on the dryer. I couldn't believe that this was the same man who had professed his love, told me he wanted me to have his son, and said that he had never loved a woman like he loved me. Walking out of the room, I left my vomit on the floor and went to the bathroom to rinse my mouth.

After wetting my entire face, I looked at my reflection in the mirror. How was I going to do this? I reached for a nearby towel, dried my face and walked out the bathroom with a plan in mind. I collected all of my findings and took them downstairs to the kitchen.

I found an empty box in the garage and threw the clothes, underwear and hair products in it. I ran upstairs and retrieved the bottle of bleach I saw in the laundry room and poured it all over the contents of the box. I contemplated about setting it on fire, but decided against it. I figured the bleach was bad enough. It would destroy all the clothes and make Kevin have to explain to Evelyn what happened to all of her hoochie wear. I placed the box in the corner of the garage underneath a sheet of newspaper. Walking back in the house, I looked at the clock and saw that it was 8:30. Kevin should be returning soon. I sat on the couch and turned on the TV to wait. Noticing the VCR, I pulled out the *1995* tape and inserted it. I sat down on the couch and pressed play on the remote control. All I could see was what looked like someone's couch, but I could also hear voices, but could not make out what was being said. Nothing could have prepared me for what I

178

was to see next. Kevin's naked body walked in plain view of the camera and lay on the couch. A beautiful naked woman that I had never seen before joined him, and got on top of him and started to ride. I was too shocked to cry. As she did her business, Kevin would say things like, "You like this big dick, baby?" and "This is the best you've ever had, isn't it?" As if that wasn't enough, a brown skinned, thick sister entered the scene and started kissing his neck and rubbing his chest. Their escapade continued for about fifteen minutes ending with all three bodies intertwined on the floor. I stopped the tape, ran to the restroom and vomited again.

Chapter Thirty-Two

The unlocking of the door woke me. I glanced at the clock and saw that it was almost 10:00. I had fallen asleep on the couch, but had my purse by my side, ready for a fast get away.

He walked in smiling, "Hey Baby," he bent down to kiss me. "Why didn't you go upstairs to lay down? You didn't have to sleep down here."

"Who's Evelyn Diggs?" I asked directly, without fear or reservation.

He paused and looked at me blankly. "She goes to the church," he answered dryly, trying to look innocent.

"Are you sleeping with her?"

"No. Why would you ask something like that?"

"Don't lie to me, Kevin." I paused and stood up and walked right up to him and added, "I'm going to ask you one more time. Are you sleeping with her?"

"No, and why are you questioning me about Sister Diggs?"

Frustrated, I walked into the garage to get my evidence and walked back into the living room.

"Okay, Kevin. Who are you sleeping with, if it's not Sister Diggs?"

"No one. What's going on with you? Have you tripped out or something?"

"Don't you dare try and turn this around to make out like I have the problem. Who the hell do these belong to?" I reached in and pulled out the bleach soaked underwear and pushed it in his face.

He slapped my hand down from his face and held my wrist tightly.

I snatched my wrist from his grasp and took a step back. "How could you?"

It was like I was looking at a stranger. My feelings exceeded betrayal. My world and future, as I knew it, were no more. A knife through the heart wouldn't hurt as much as the sheer pain I was experiencing. I wanted to hurt him, as I was hurt. I wanted him to feel the pain and agony I was feeling. I drew back my hand and with all the force and misery behind it, I hit him in the face.

His head jerked to the side, where it stayed for a moment, stunned at what I had done. He rubbed his hand on the area of contact and then examined his hand for signs of blood. There was none. A part of me wished there was. He turned and slowly looked at me. I braced myself, not knowing if this stranger in front of me was capable of hitting back. Instead he stepped towards me and put his arms around me, holding me close to him. The comfort of his chest and the smell of his cologne weakened me. I remembered the security and love it had given me, but the feeling quickly faded; I struggled free from his arms, realizing it was all a lie. Nothing was like it was and never would be.

"We need to talk, Natalie."

"Talk." I paused. "Talk about what. Let's see, let's talk about you sleeping with members of your church, one who happens to be calling my apartment all hours of the night and hanging up. Let's talk about the sex tape I found in your closet." I reached for the tape I had hidden in the couch cushions and waved it in the air. "Maybe we should have a conversation about this sorry ass, pitiful excuse of a ring you bought me, never intending to marry me. It probably is identical to the one that's on Shelby's finger. By the way she called me last night!" I said as I took the ring off my finger and then searched his face for any remorse, and added, "No, we need to talk about the STD you gave me and the fact I'm carrying your baby — again! You choose. Which one would you like to talk about?"

He was silent as though he was trying to take in all of what was said. Then he had the nerve to say, "Calm down, Natalie. Let me talk."

I screamed, "Hell, no. Why should I calm down? To hear more lies? For Christ sake, you're a Goddamn preacher. You're supposed to be a man of God!"

"I am a man of God. Nobody is perfect. We have all fallen short of the grace of God, I'm no exception."

I interrupted, "Stop it with that 'fallen short' act. That's your excuse for everything. I know I didn't go to seminary school, but realizing no one is perfect doesn't give you the right to do all the outright sinful things you've done. The worse part is, you don't have an ounce of remorse."

His facial features hardened. "So you're gonna try and tell me how I feel," he said in a cold tone. "Okay, you are so holy now. Why don't you leave? That's what you're gonna do anyway, right? Just leave, since I'm so bad."

He had the nerve to turn hard on me. Talk about flipping the script. He just stood looking at me with a blank expression, waiting for me to make a move. I struggled to keep the tears in. I wasn't going to give him the satisfaction. I reached down, picked up my purse and walked toward the door, not looking back.

As I walked toward my car, I could no longer contain the tears. A few seconds later, I was down the block. Before turning off his street, I looked in my rear view mirror and realized he didn't even try to stop me from leaving.

Chapter Thirty-Three

Janet looked at me dumbfounded. She then picked up her empty coffee cup and said, "I'm so sorry. I hate you had to experience that." She then added, "But you know, maybe it was a blessing you did."

"I know. That's what I've been telling myself. I just can't believe I've been so stupid."

"Don't do that to yourself. He's the one at fault, not you. He's the one that took you for a ride. He's going to have to stand accountable for all of this. Just be glad you know now."

"I know, but why did I have to go through all of this madness before I found out?"

"There's a reason for everything, Sweetie. Just don't be like so many other women and let him talk you back into his life," she said in a motherly tone.

"No. I won't. He hasn't even bothered to call and apologize," I said sadly.

"You don't need him to. You just be strong, you know what you've got to do. Just lick your wounds and move on. It's not going to be easy, but you've got to. And by all means, don't call him."

"I won't. I can't."

I hadn't felt like coming in to the office at all, but I had to let Janet know what happened in Chicago and check on things. I had purposely waited until the guys were in the field before coming in. I was dressed in jeans and a t-shirt. I couldn't even motivate myself to put on makeup.

I noticed a message that Harry Bell had called and for me to call him immediately. What now? I just wanted to go home and go to sleep, but I picked up the receiver to call him to find out what was so urgent.

After the initial small talk, Harry told me that the client was very pleased with all the hard work my office had put into the new test market we were spearheading. He said that Telo.Com was very impressed with our numbers and wanted to expand in the Texas market. They wanted me to oversee the project in Dallas and would pay for relocation with a $3,000 bonus.

"You're kidding, right?" This was almost too much to bear.

"No, I'm not. They want you there next week. Their relocation department will find you an apartment in the heart of downtown." Harry said, sounding impressed that they were willing to go all out to close the deal. "You can hand the NY office over to Christopher, he's ready for full management. I can guarantee you will make an override of sixty-five cents off every unit sold out of the New York office for as long as it's in business."

"That's good to hear. I've worked too hard to just walk away empty handed. But, next week, Harry?" I said in disbelief.

"Yep, they need to make an early hit, due to the deregulation. We've got people down there tomorrow signing papers for the space. So, if you don't want the gig, we are up a creek. They want you, only you. This will be big for the company, Natalie. We can count on you, right?"

My head was swimming a mile a minute. I was definitely in a major depression and maybe this was the change I needed. I just didn't have the passion for the responsibility of starting something so significant. I couldn't even motivate myself to come into the office on time. Did I have it in me to be on top of my game for who knows how long? I had worked so hard to establish this office to the point that it could run without me. Was I up for the challenge, after everything I'd been through?

On the other hand, a move might be what I needed. My best friends and family were in Dallas and they were what I needed, more than anything. There was nothing left for me in New York except bad memories of Kevin. A new start would bring on a new life. It would allow me to be so busy that I couldn't think of anything else, except the challenge of opening the office.

Before I knew it, I heard, "Yes, I'm in. But instead of $3,000, I want $10,000. Is that a deal?" I figured what the hell did I have to lose? I had already established an office where everything was running smoothly and I had an Assistant Manager I personally trained. If they really needed me, they needed to come with it.

"Natalie, I'm gonna have to get back with you on that. I don't have the authority to approve that amount."

"Okay, do what you need to do, but $10,000 is the price. Let me know."

Ten minutes later, I was $10,000 richer.

Chapter Thirty-Four

There were moving boxes everywhere. The packing process was taking longer than I had hoped for, mainly because I was spending a lot of time in bed, tired. I didn't know if it was the pregnancy or the depression. I just couldn't shake it. I started packing and then had to lay down for a nap. My thoughts were still centered on Kevin. I questioned my worth as a woman. I wondered if I had the qualities that could satisfy any man enough to be faithful. I struggled with thoughts of the abortion I had to undergo tomorrow.

I missed Kevin. My thoughts envisioned him making love to the women on the tape. I could see his hands rubbing over their bodies similar to the way his hands rubbed my own. I wondered if anything between us had been genuine. I wondered if he ever loved me at all. Would any man ever want me enough to want to marry me?

I walked in the bathroom for a Kleenex and noticed my reflection in the mirror. I looked ugly. I was in agony and didn't want to live. The pain was just too much to bear. I couldn't go to Dallas and spearhead anything. I didn't have it in me. I looked in the medicine cabinet and pulled out a bottle of Tylenol PM. I opened it and poured the entire contents in my hand. I took one more look at the disgusting image in the mirror, took a deep breath and swallowed the pills.

I went to the living room and sat down. All of a sudden fear pierced my body, after realizing what I had just done. I didn't want to die. I just didn't want to live. I jumped off the couch and called Janet and told her what I had done.

"You did what!!!!" I heard a dial tone. Less than ten minutes later, I heard an ambulance and then a knocking at the door. I opened it and it was the paramedics.

The paramedics rushed in through the open door and started taking my vital signs and asking me questions. I was so sleepy. After awhile, I couldn't make out what was going on or what was being said.

"I'm sorry. I don't know why I did it." Hearing my own words, I felt like I was speaking in slow motion. Then there was darkness.

I woke up in the hospital. The doctor came in and said that I would be released in the morning. I was relieved because I had my abortion scheduled for 2:00 in the afternoon. I was determined for nothing to stand in the way of that.

After the doctor left the hospital room, I heard weeping in the corner of the room. I saw the woman that had always shown so much strength in tears. Janet's back was facing the bed.

"Janet, what's wrong?" I felt awful that I was the cause of her tears. "I'm okay. I'm sorry I got you so involved in all my mess."

"I can't be the person you need me to be. I'm not that strong. Natalie, you've been through a lot and you need someone that can minister to you on the level you need." She wept. "I don't want to lose you. I'm sure if I had been through everything that you've been through, I may have tried to take my own life, too."

I interrupted, "I didn't want to die, Janet. I just didn't have the strength to go on." I wanted desperately to reassure her.

"I know. I know, Sweetie, that's why I want you to talk to my pastor."

"Your pastor?" I repeated, amazed that she would have the nerve to put any "man of God" in front of me.

"Yes, Natalie. I've already called him and he wants to meet with you. He said he had time tomorrow."

"You know what I have planned tomorrow, and the next day I leave for Texas." I explained, not wanting to open up to anyone, especially another preacher. In my opinion they were all manipulative, money-hungry womanizers who used the Bible for their own personal gain.

"Your procedure is in the afternoon. We can meet with him afterwards."

"Afterwards! Janet, I'm not going to be in the mood to talk to anyone after the abortion," I tried to explain.

"We'll wait three or four hours and he can meet us at your place. By then your painkillers would have set in." Janet looked at me and put her hand on my arm. "Please, Nat, do it for me. I need to know that you are leaving New York with your head on straight. I don't want anything to happen to you."

My heart weakened. Her words were very sincere. "Okay, okay. You win." I paused. "Janet, for the record, you don't have to worry about me committing suicide. I know that's not the answer."

"I know, Sweetie. I know."

Chapter Thirty-Five

I raised my tear-streaked face from the soaked pillow and opened my swollen eye lids and looked around the dark room. I thought I heard someone knock. "Janet," I yelled.

"Yeah, Natalie. Reverend Perry is here." I could hear the door unlocking, then an unfamiliar male voice.

I was not in the mood to be counseled. I was not in much pain, but I was very drowsy. I figured this guy was going to try and pray my problems away. I just wasn't feeling the whole idea. All I wanted was sleep.

They didn't come in my bedroom right away. Instead, I could hear slight whispers of words I couldn't make out. She was probably filling him in on all the drama of the past year. I sat up and adjusted the pillow behind me for support. I rubbed my hands through my hair with the attempt to look a bit more presentable. I reached over and grabbed the Chap Stick from my nightstand. My lips were so dry they felt cracked. When I made an attempt to stand up to turn on the lamp, I could feel blood release from my vagina onto the heavy pad between my legs. Taken by surprise, I sat back down, feeling nasty, violated, and empty.

"Natalie, are you decent? Reverend Perry and I would like to come in," Janet said in a mellow voice outside the door.

I raised my legs back on top of the bed and covered them with the sheet. "Yes, come on in." I hoped he wouldn't take too long. I didn't feel like talking about all the personal details of the past several months with anyone, especially not a stranger, definitely not a preacher.

Janet walked in with a short, balding man who was about forty. He had a pleasant face and genuine smile.

"Natalie, this is Reverend Perry." She introduced us as they both approached the foot of my queen-sized bed.

"Sister Natalie. It is a pleasure to meet you." He extended his small brown hand to mine. He was dressed in a blue and white Nike jogging suit and tennis shoes. "Janet has told me so much about you..."

"I bet she has." I interrupted and cut my eye to Janet.

"She has told me about your storms, but she mainly told me about your spirit and your heart." He was looking directly into my eyes.

I made eye contact with Janet who was smiling softly at me. "I have to say, I don't know what I would have done without Janet. She's been a true friend."

"Natalie, I don't want to stay too long. I'm aware you have had a rough day, but I would like to start off with praying for you. Would that be okay?"

"Yes, that will be okay."

Janet sat on the foot of the bed becoming the link to allow all of us to join hands. "Heavenly Father, we welcome you in this place. We need you, Father, to come in and bless us with your needed grace and mercy. Lord, we come before you, first to say thank you for your many blessings. Sometimes I know we cannot see the blessings behind the burdens, but reveal it, Lord, when it is your will. Let us see your will for our lives through all of this." His grip was getting firmer. "Lord, touch Natalie's body and heal her womb." I then felt Janet release my hand and place it gently on my belly. "We rebuke any evil spirits, Lord, and in the name of Jesus, we cast them out and restore her to be whole." His loud and authoritative tone of his voice sent shivers down my spine. "Cleanse her of everything that's not you, Father."

I could hear Janet say a few, "Yes, Fathers" and "Hallelujahs."

"Lord, your child has been through the fire. Restore her faith in men, ministry, and in you, Lord. Speak a sacred sermon that heals her spirit and restores her soul. " His voice softened and he started speaking in tongue. All of a sudden my closed eyes started to burn and fill with tears.

"Holy Father, touch her, heal her, keep her by your side. And as she heals, Lord, have her grow more in you, Lord. As her body is strengthened, strengthen her connection with you, Lord. Take away the pain, both physically and emotionally and give her an overwhelming peace in her spirit. In your Son Jesus Christ's name we give all the glory to God. Amen."

I wiped my face with my hands, which were traced with tears. I looked up to see Janet whose face and eyes were red. She went to the bathroom where I heard the sounds of her blowing her nose. When she came back in she hugged Reverend Perry.

"Thank you, Reverend Perry. I feel better." I was still hurt emotionally, and of course, physically, but I had a peace that everything was going to be okay. I took the opportunity to ask a question I just had to know. "Can I ask you a question, Reverend Perry?"

"Anything," he said kneeling beside my bed.

"How can I truly ever trust in a relationship, if the man I loved couldn't be faithful and he was a pastor of a church? I mean if a man of God can't be faithful, then how can I be sure any man can? How do I learn to trust? How do I get through this?" I had more questions, but I had started to get more emotional as each question was released from my lips.

"You have been through things that would make most people go crazy and look at you — you are still standing. You have already made it through. The first step is to be thankful for the grace the Lord has given you to guide you through. You are a strong woman. Give glory to God for that."

Janet interrupted, "That's what I keep telling her. She doesn't know how strong and blessed she is."

"I need you to pray for a spirit of discernment. That will allow you to be able to see and detect things about a person's character they are not putting out for people to see. The Lord will allow you to see them for the people they really are. There are plenty of wolves in sheep's clothing out there, but the spirit of discernment will allow you to see them for who they really are," Reverend Perry explained.

"That's so true, Reverend. I had that same feeling when I met Kevin. A feeling that something just wasn't right about him. My feelings only elevated from bad to worse when Natalie told me all the things he had put her through.

"Exactly. Some people call it a sixth sense or woman's intuition. It's nothing but God, trying to reveal something to you." He was speaking in such a calming voice that soothed me and allowed me to relax and be receptive to what he was saying. "Most importantly, pray daily. Pray for the Holy Spirit to guide you through every aspect of your life. Talk to the Lord, ask him questions, he'll answer."

"That's right, he sure will." Janet said.

"You now have a pocket overflowing with wisdom, use it. Don't allow what you have been through to be in vain."

"I won't."

"Always remember you made it through all of that mess because God has a plan for you, greater than you could ever imagine. The devil tried to destroy you, but no weapon formed against you shall prosper. Know that. Believe that with all your heart. Because through your belief, lies your blessing."

I felt energized, like the weight of the past week had been lifted. Prayer was powerful and I was going to be okay. It would be a process, but I knew I could get over this and move on. I realized that just like all men were not the same, all preachers weren't either.

Reverend Perry had been happily married for the past eight years. He and his wife had two boys and were anxiously looking forward to the birth of their daughter in February. He shared that he had known some people in churches throughout the years that were more in the world than in the spirit. He confided that was not the majority.

"Churches are the reflection of the world. If there are sinful and trifling people in the world, you are going to have a percentage of that in the church, after all, the mission of the church is to minister to them and bring them into a more Christ-like existence." He paused, "It's just a shame when the shepherd is one. But you are going to be okay."

Reverend Perry got his balance and stood from the squatting position he had been in while ministering to me.

I slowly stood up and prepared to walk him to the door, realizing he had a family to get home to. I was so thankful for his coming. It's funny that what I dreaded the most turned out to be the greatest blessing for me.

"Thanks for coming, Reverend," Janet said as she hugged him goodbye as we approached the door.

"Not a problem. It was my pleasure."

"I can't thank you enough. I can't describe how much better I feel," I said while hugging him.

"God bless you, Sister," he said and walked out the door.

I closed the door and walked over to Janet and said, " Thank you for that. I really needed it."

"Girl, I had to. I needed to know you would be okay. You needed to be lifted up in prayer."

"I know. Thanks again for everything. Not just for Reverend Perry, but for everything." I struggled to articulate my feelings to my secretary that had become my best friend and in many ways saved my life. I cleared my throat and fought the tears. "Janet, you've been such a blessing to me. I'm going to miss you."

"I'm going to miss you, too. Listen, I'm gonna go. I'll call tomorrow before the movers get here. You have a big day tomorrow, so I'm gonna let you get some sleep."

We hugged and she walked out the door.

"Hey, Janet," I said as she looked back, "I love you."

"I love you, too."

As I returned to my bed to relish in my peaceful spirit, the phone rang. Not feeling like talking to anyone, I looked at the Caller ID. It was Kevin. After days, he had decided to call. I smiled, walked right on by, got in my bed and went to sleep. My new life started tomorrow and it had no room for the past.